"I challenge you, Morton," Ron said with a sneer.

Chris shrugged his shoulders. "To what?"

"A race, what do you think? My Raiders against the High-Fives."

"What's that going to prove?" Alex questioned.

"No one asked you, Alex, but it'll prove who's the best skier, that's what."

"We don't have to prove anything," Stretch grinned. "We know we're good."

"Then put up or shut up," Ron added quietly.

"You're on," Chris said confidently.

"Okay, first group to have everyone down at the bottom—with their skis on—wins."

J.R. looked at the slope and felt his throat drop into his stomach. . . .

THE HIGH-FIVES ™

SKIING FOR THE PRIZE

S.S. Gorman

A MINSTREL® BOOK

PUBLISHED BY POCKET BOOKS

New York   London   Toronto   Sydney   Tokyo   Singapore

A MINSTREL PAPERBACK *ORIGINAL*

A Minstrel Book published by
POCKET BOOKS, a division of Simon & Schuster Inc.
1230 Avenue of the Americas, New York, NY 10020

Copyright © 1992 by Susan Schaumberg Gorman
Front cover illustration by Bryce Lee

ISBN: 0-671-74501-8

First Minstrel Books printing January 1992

10 9 8 7 6 5 4 3 2

A MINSTREL BOOK and colophon are registered trademarks
of Simon & Schuster Inc.

Printed in the U.S.A.

For my father, the human rope tow,
Edward George Schaumberg
who first taught me to ski.

Special thanks to
Jack Hyland

SKIING
FOR THE
PRIZE

Chapter 1

LET IT SNOW, LET IT SNOW, LET IT SNOW

"This is going to be the best ski season ever," blue-eyed Chris Morton said, hoisting his Head XR skis over his right shoulder. He tried to balance the skis as he zipped up the new red ski jacket he'd gotten for Christmas.

"Yeah," Stretch Evans answered, following along to Chris's dad's blue van. Stretch was Chris's best friend. "The radio said most of the ski areas have a snow base of at least forty-four inches."

"And that's real snow, not man-made," Gadget Shaw, the gang's resident genius, emphasized. He jogged to catch up with Chris and Stretch while pushing up his wire-rimmed glasses. He'd tried contact lenses, but liked glasses better. Dumping his skis, he took out the group's blue spiral notebook that he regularly kept facts in and jotted down the snowfall figures.

1

Chris slid his skis and Gadget's boots into the back of the van. "I can't wait another minute. I've got to hit the slopes." He shook his blond wavy hair. "I've been practicing in my ski boots around the basement for weeks."

Stretch jumped into the backseat next to Gadget. "I hear ya. My mom says if I bring my ski poles into the house once more, I have to live on the back porch." Stretch's dark brown eyes gleamed with mischief. "I keep telling her I need to practice mogul jumping. Moguls are the bumps on the ski run, Gadget."

"I may not know how to do everything, but I do know the correct terminology for it all," Gadget said, not really insulted.

"Parents just don't understand. I'm aching to pound those hills. The two times my family's gone haven't been enough," Chris said, jumping into the front seat.

Gadget sighed. "My mother's sure I'm going to break a leg."

"That's funny," Stretch said, chuckling. "Your folks are doctors, they should know most skiers don't break any bones."

"Try to explain that to my mom," Gadget said, clicking his seat belt on. "My mother doesn't think of me as a normal skier."

Chris leaned over the back of the front seat to rumple Gadget's sandy hair. "Ah, her precious little boy," he said in baby talk.

Stretch joined in, cooing. "I guess that's what happens when you're an only child."

"Give me a break, you two," Gadget said, trying not

to laugh. "My mom thinks I'm a klutz, and she hates it when I ski."

Stretch shrugged his shoulders. "Then how come she let you join the Downhillers Ski Club?"

"She figures it's a safe alternative. You know, a group that teaches you ski safety and how to ski. Besides, they don't have to drive me all the way to the slopes. They just have to get me to the bus on time."

Chris slapped the back of his seat and whooped suddenly, unable to contain his excitement another minute. "Five straight Saturdays of hotdogging and bombing."

"Five weeks of snow plows and stem christies is more like it." Gadget knew that most of his time would be spent practicing different techniques for stopping and turning.

"Not with good equipment and slope time," Chris argued. "This ski swap night is really cool. I've decided I'm coming home with K-2 skis, preferably with Marker bindings, Atomic ARF boots and maybe some new ski poles."

"You're cracked," Stretch said as he crossed his long, lanky legs. "Why would anyone try to unload top of the line equipment?"

"Actually my stuff's just a little old, that's all. I'd settle for some Hart Super Lites with graphics and Salomon bindings."

Stretch shook his head. "No one's going to get rid of those either."

Chris shrugged and turned forward to stare out at the stars.

"Are the Klipp brothers going to be there tonight?" Stretch asked.

"They said they'd meet us," Gadget answered. "J.R.'s been talking about it all week."

"He claims he's grown a foot over the last year and has to get longer skis and new boots," Chris added.

"I told him to hang on to his old skis. I wouldn't give up my shorties for nothing." Stretch uncrossed his legs and leaned forward, anxious to get moving.

"You know, if your skis are too long you really can get stuck between the moguls," Chris said, agreeing.

"I don't think either of the Klipps have to worry about having super-long skis too soon," Gadget said. "Jack's the shortest seventh grader at Dugan Junior High, and J.R.'s got to be one of the smallest sixth graders at Bressler Elementary."

"Don't remind them," Chris said, "especially Jack."

"Being short's no big deal," Gadget said. "No pun intended."

Stretch rolled down the window and puffed little white clouds of warm breath into the cold night air. "I still wouldn't mention it, especially now that you've grown so much."

Chris checked his watch. "I wonder what's keeping my dad? We're going to be late."

Right then Mr. Morton, a tall, muscular man, stepped off the porch of his ranch-style home. He opened the door of the van and slipped into the front seat. "Let's say we skip the Downhillers meeting, and just head for the slopes."

"All right," Stretch cheered.

4

"You've got my vote, Dad," Chris added.

Gadget cleared his throat. "I'd better phone my parents and get permission first."

Frank Morton grinned at Gadget. "I'm just kidding, William—sorry, I mean Gadget."

"That's all right, Mr. Morton. My real name is William Irving Shaw, but even my dad calls me Gadget. He thought up the name."

"I was only kidding you about the skiing. But in just a week you boys will be going skiing every Saturday."

"Yes," Chris cheered. "But we've got to get to the Downhillers meeting tonight so we can sign up for the bus."

Mr. Morton turned the key. "I can take a hint. Next stop, the YMCA for the Downhillers Club and the swap night." He backed out of the driveway and headed down a tree-lined street in Conrad, Colorado.

Signs of the holiday season still lingered. It was January fifth, and a few golden garlands and red and green lights still decorated the trees and houses. Soon it would all be replaced with blankets of snow. Conrad was a small college town, full of activities and young families. It had been mild that winter in town, but the mountains had gotten lots of snow since the resort areas opened Thanksgiving weekend.

Mr. Morton turned the van into the parking lot of the new YMCA. "You sure you don't want me to come in and check out the equipment with you, Chris?"

"Positive, Dad. I know what I'm looking for." Chris leaped out of the van and opened the back to get his skis.

5

"I don't get it, Morton," Stretch whispered as he gave Chris a hand. "Your dad runs the coolest sporting goods store in town. How come you can't get your equipment there, for free?"

Chris glared at the lanky black boy. "Stretch, how long have I known you? You know my dad. No freebies. Even with the family discount, I can't afford new K-2's. Believe me, I've tried."

"Bummer," Stretch added, and slammed the back door shut.

Mr. Morton waved to the trio as they headed for the door. "Meet you guys here at nine."

"Right, Dad."

Gadget pushed open the heavy double doors of the YMCA, where the High-Fives had played basketball last year and where the Downhillers met. The lobby was full of kids carrying skis, boots, and poles. The walls were plastered with Olympic posters and the hottest skiing stars like the Mahre brothers, Tiger Shaw, and Felix McGrath. The smell of hot apple cider filled the air. Long tables were set up against the redbrick walls and were heaped with doughnuts and sweet rolls.

"All right," Stretch cried. "Food. Let's grab some goodies."

"Not yet," Chris said, clutching a handful of Stretch's navy down jacket. "We've got to go down to the gym and put my equipment up for grabs."

Stretch grinned. "Oh, all right. I guess you won't be happy until you unload that stuff." He snatched one jelly doughnut from the table and jogged after Chris and

Gadget. "Hey, maybe *I* should buy them just to get you to relax."

"Where's the fire, guys?" Alex Tye, a tall, thin girl with green eyes, flipped her long blond braid over her shoulder. She held a pair of Dynafit ski boots. "Wait up, Gadget." She caught up with the boys on the stairs and they entered the gym together.

Chris stopped short to catch his breath. The gymnasium had been transformed into the largest ski shop he'd ever seen. Rows of racks had been set up and were now lined with all sizes and styles of skis and poles. The next row was filled with boots, everything from toddler sizes to adults. The far side of the gym looked like a department store. Tables were filled with hats, gloves, mittens, and goggles. There were also hangers crammed with all kinds of ski clothes—sweaters, bibs, stretch pants, and jackets. If it was used for skiing, it was there.

"Wow," Chris said. "There's more stuff here than at my dad's place."

Stretch leaned against the door jamb. "I didn't know this many people in Conrad skied."

"It's like this every year," Alex said flippantly. "Haven't you ever been to one of these before?"

"Well, sure, a few years ago, but I was more interested in the doughnuts then." Chris shook his head, still in shock.

Stretch dug in his pocket for change. "I wish I'd brought my stuff to sell. I think I'll call my dad to see if he can bring it down."

Chris rubbed his hands together. "I feel lucky tonight.

Suddenly Jack Klipp, a small but athletic-looking boy with wavy, dark brown hair, and squinty brown eyes, rushed over to the gang. "Hey, I hope you guys have signed up for the ski bus. They didn't expect such a big turnout and they're running out of space already. They're talking about adding more buses, but the new ones wouldn't start going until the middle of February."

"Quit clowning, Jack," Stretch said, chuckling.

"Get real, Evans." Jack sneered at Stretch. "I wouldn't joke about a thing like this."

Chris's face showed instant panic. He shoved his ski equipment against Jack's shoulder and made a beeline for the club's sign-up sheet. "We could blow this whole thing."

"Wait for me," Stretch said, chasing after him.

"I'm right behind you," Gadget added, and dumped his ski boots on top of the tower in Jack's already over-loaded arms.

"Hey, do I look like a locker," Jack grumbled, and the boots fell to the floor. "Find J.R.," he yelled after them. "He's holding a place in line for you." After Jack bent down to pick up the boots, he noticed Alex standing beside him. "So aren't you signing up?"

"It was the first thing I did when I walked in the door," she answered.

"Well then, give me a hand with this junk." Jack

handed her Chris's poles and they fumbled awkwardly with the rest of the stuff.

"I don't see him anywhere." Chris's voice was high and anxious sounding as he shuffled through the crowd trying to spot J.R. in the sign-up line.

"He shouldn't be this hard to spot," Gadget said, squinting his hazel-colored eyes behind his glasses. "But everywhere I look I see short kids with brown eyes, straight dark hair, and freckles. And they're all wearing orange ski jackets."

Chris grunted as he elbowed his way closer to the banner that read Downhillers Club. "If he were taller, it'd be easier to see him." Chris was starting to panic. "When did everybody in town get so tall?"

"They didn't," Gadget said. "You're used to being with a group of students all relatively the same size. Now that you're outside Dugan Junior High, there's a much wider selection of heights. . . ."

"Not now," Chris pleaded. "If we don't get on this bus, we won't be able to go skiing next Saturday. I want the High-Fives to be together."

"Over here. Over here," J. R. Klipp's high voice pierced the low droning of the crowd.

Stretch pinpointed the spot where the sixth grader's voice was coming from, and the trio elbowed their way through a mass of people in coats, hats, and winter gear. "Boy, are we glad to see you."

Chris slapped him a high-five. "Thanks a lot, man, you saved our necks." He counted the people in front of J.R. "Any idea how many spots are left on the bus?"

9

J.R. shook his head. "They announced a little while ago that they're filling up the last bus now."

"We've just got to get on it." Stretch emphasized the point by slamming his fist into his other hand.

"It won't be any fun if the High-Fives aren't together." J.R. looked worried. "These guys are from my school," he added, pointing to two boys in front of him. "They're holding places for you, too."

"What a terrific idea," Gadget said.

"Thanks a lot, guys," Stretch said, high-fiving the two boys. They stepped out of line, and Gadget, Stretch, and Chris slipped in.

"Hey, what's going on up there? No cuts."

Chris turned to face Ron Porter, the class bully, who stood a head taller than Chris. His bright red hair and intense blue eyes were intimidating. As usual, he was flanked by his buddies, a mangy group that called themselves the Raiders. "Just relax, Porter," Chris said boldly. "We're not taking cuts. J.R. and his two friends were holding our spots. There were three guys ahead of you before, and there are three guys ahead of you now. What's the dif?"

"The dif is, it's you, Morton," husky Randy Salazar added.

"Besides it's illegal," Peter Farrell whined. Chris thought he was a real idiot.

"It's not illegal," Stretch said. "There aren't any rules."

"Then there should be," Greg Forbes said, shaking his jet black hair.

"Besides, there aren't three of you—there are four

of you in line now." Ron's massive, freckled face burned red with anger.

For a moment Chris thought they were doomed. "So, uh—"

"So, I've already signed up." J.R. said, stepping out of the line. "Three places, three spaces."

"All right," Stretch shouted.

"That was close," Gadget whispered in Stretch's ear.

"I hear you," Stretch whispered back.

Ron and the rest of the Raiders mumbled because they knew there was nothing they could do. "Well, you'd better pray we get on this last bus, Morton. If we don't, you're going to pay for it all year long."

Chris ignored him, but felt his stomach do flip-flops. He wanted to go skiing more than anything, but he didn't want to start the new year off with Ron Porter and the Raiders on his back. "Here we go again."

Chapter 2

THE SWAP

"So what happened? Are you in?" Jack shouted when the guys rejoined him.

"Just barely." Stretch sighed.

"Yes, thanks to you and J.R., and your quick thinking," Gadget added.

"We were in the last group of ten to make it." Chris patted J.R. on the back for thanks.

"Yes, and Ron Porter and his friends were numbers six through ten," Gadget continued.

Jack grumbled. "Looks like we'll be stuck with their ugly faces."

"Who cares as long as we're together," Chris interrupted. "We may have been the last ten to make the sign-up, but they don't assign seats so we won't have to ride the same bus or ski on the same slopes."

"Chris is right. We're not going to let them ruin our Saturdays," Stretch cheered.

"Heck, I'm not even going to let them spoil tonight,"

Chris continued. "I'm going to find my new skis." Chris marched up to the swap shop table and began filling out his cards.

"If you have any questions about how our silent auction works, feel free to ask," Nora Tye, Alex's mother, said, handing Chris two big yellow tags.

"Thanks, Mrs. Tye." Chris smiled at her. The tags had a number across the top, with the same number on the side next to a perforated edge. Chris tore off the second number and stuck it in his pocket. "Let's hope number eighty-four is lucky," he mumbled. He filled out the larger part of the tag with a description of his skis, bindings, and poles. He did the same for his boots on the other tag. The Klipps hurriedly scribbled their information for their skis, and Gadget did the same for his boots.

"They're starting a ski film in the auditorium in ten minutes," Stretch announced as he sauntered back from the ski-wear tables. "Let's go get seats."

"You guys go ahead," Chris said. "I want to check out the stuff to see if there's anything worth bidding on."

"Wait until after the movie," J.R. pleaded.

"You've got time to do that later," Jack added.

"Besides, no one's supposed to be looking now, anyway," Alex reminded him.

"Yeah, so come on," Jack said, leading the way toward the exit. "I'll tell ya right now, I'm not saving you a seat." The rest of the High-Fives headed for the door. Chris looked over his shoulder and sighed. He reluctantly followed.

"There are some seats down there," Gadget said, spying an open clump on the left side of the auditorium.

"Let's nab 'em." Jack darted ahead.

"See you guys later," Alex said, and went to join a group of girls from school.

Stretch swiveled around to stare at the crowd. "Everybody's here. I'll bet there's not one kid from Dugan Junior High at home tonight."

"There are lots of kids from Bressler, too," J.R. chimed in.

"Who cares about sixth graders," Jack said, and lightly punched his younger brother on the shoulder.

"Give the kid a break," Stretch said, and proceeded to punch J.R. on the other shoulder.

"We were in elementary school just last year," Gadget reminded them.

"Yeah, but what a difference a year makes." Jack tousled his brother's hair and side-stepped away and into the row of seats Gadget had spotted earlier.

"Hey, there are coats and stuff on the back of these chairs," Stretch declared.

"And there's a good reason for them, too." Greg Forbes, who was sitting in the row behind the High-Fives, leaned forward and put his arms on the back of one of the seats. He glared at Stretch. "We don't want our coats to get all scrunched up."

"Too bad," Jack blasted. He picked up Hank Thompson's dark green jacket, ski hat, scarf, and gloves and dumped them in Hank's lap in the seat directly behind him.

"What's the big idea?" chubby Hank asked.

14

The other High-Fives mimicked Jack's movements and dumped the other coats back into the hands of the Raiders. Unlucky Chris had Ron sitting directly behind him.

"What do you think you're doing?" Ron bellowed.

"Sitting down to watch a Warren Miller skiing video," Chris answered, without looking at the redhead.

"My stuff was there," Ron said as he stood up.

"Not anymore," Chris murmured.

"Look," Gadget said tactfully, "there aren't enough open seats for anyone to waste them on coats."

"Want to bet?" Randy Salazar stood, ready to pick a fight, but the lights dimmed just then and the Raiders all sat and gave up reluctantly.

Chris tingled as the screen filled with a snow-white slope dotted with expert skiers challenging the fall line in a race to the bottom. The crowd whistled and shouted. Chris wasn't the only one excited by ski season. For the next half hour the High-Fives lost themselves in a spectacular exhibition of downhill racers, stunt skiers, jumpers, and slalom racers. When the lights came up, each boy knew in his heart that he could ski as well as any performer on the screen.

"That was totally cool," Stretch said, standing in front of his seat.

"I want to try one of those snow boards," Jack said. "It looks like surfing on the snow."

"Theoretically, it should be very similar," Gadget added.

"You'll never know." Ron chuckled from the row behind. "It's a lot harder than it looks. I know, I tried it last year."

15

"Me, too," Greg chimed in. "And believe me, none of you wimps could make it down half a slope on a board."

"Unless it's in a toboggan headed for the first aid station," Randy said, laughing loud at his own joke.

"We'll see about that," Jack snapped back.

"It does look hard," J.R. said nervously.

"You'd better stick to the beginner's hill then," Ron said in baby talk. The Raiders all laughed as if Ron were truly funny. Then they picked up their coats and shuffled out of the row.

"What did you say that for?" Jack snapped at J.R.

"It's the truth, snow boarding looks hard," J.R. cried.

"Don't worry about it, J.R." Gadget said, putting a hand on the younger Klipp's shoulder. "Just stick to skis."

"As long as you can keep up with the rest of us. Now let's get back to the auction." Chris was in a hurry and slid past the others and marched back to the gym.

"I'm getting something to eat," Stretch said, catching hold of J.R.'s sleeve. "Doughnuts, cider—après ski, I think they call it."

J.R. laughed. "Yeah, but we didn't ski."

"So, we're practicing in reverse," Stretch answered back. "Eat first, ski Saturday."

Chris shuffled through the crowded gym and meticulously evaluated all the skis, poles, and boots that were up for auction. He wasn't impressed.

"Find anything you can't live without?" Jack asked.

Chris turned around, a little startled to see Jack.

"Not really. Most of this stuff is worse than mine—it's junk."

"Did you really think you were going to find K-2's? I mean, really. They're top of the line. No one's going to unload them here."

"I guess not." Chris leaned on a rack and fiddled with the leather strap of a pole. "It's just that I wanted them so bad."

"You'll get them. Maybe not tonight, but you'll get them."

"I hope so." He peered around the end of the aisle. "I haven't given up yet."

"Mind if I hang out with you?"

Chris shrugged. "Maybe you'll spot something I don't see." Just as the words tumbled out of his mouth, Chris spied a pair of skis poised at the end of the row. "Hey, aren't those Kneissl Graphic Magics?" The boys bolted to the spot and Chris picked them off the rack.

"Hey, I think you're right."

"They're the perfect length for me, one eighties."

Jack picked up the other ski. "Not too many gouges on the bottom, either."

"Solomon bindings, too. I like that."

"I think this model came out about two years ago."

"A good year for skis," Chris said, and allowed himself to grin. He was starting to feel optimistic. "Maybe it will be my lucky night."

"What about the poles?" Jack held them horizontally and glanced down the length to see if they were bowed.

"Not bad, not bad," Chris said, going through the same motions as the older Klipp.

"I'm going to bid for them."

"Go for it," Jack added, almost as excited as Chris.

"Do you think fifty bucks will do it?"

"No way, they go for over a hundred in the stores."

Chris looked glum. "I don't have a hundred bucks. Besides, they're used." He paused. "How much have you got?"

"Why do you want to know?" Jack took out his wallet and flipped it open.

Chris nabbed it from him. "Twenty-five dollars, plus my fifty, that makes seventy-five dollars."

"Hold on." Jack grabbed for the wallet but Chris held on.

"That's my money. What am I supposed to bid with?"

"Please, Jack. If I bid seventy-five, I could get them."

Jack took his wallet back. "But you don't have seventy-five dollars, so you'd better hope that fifty dollars is enough."

"I'll pay you back as soon as I can," Chris pleaded.

"Yeah, and when will that be? When you're sixty?"

"Come on, Jack, please."

"Sorry, pal." Jack stuffed the wallet into his back pocket. "Maybe one of the other guys can help you. I'm out of here." He shot around the rack.

Chris clutched the equipment. He was afraid if he set it back on the rack, someone else would spot his find. He wanted to make sure his bid would be the only bid. He checked carefully and then tucked the equipment behind two pairs of skis at the end of the aisle. He walked to the left and then back to the right, to double check his hiding spot. It was the best he could do. Just then he spotted J.R. coming his way.

"J.R., ol' buddy, ol' pal," Chris said. "How's it going?" He put his arm around J.R.'s shoulder and gave it a squeeze.

"Fine, just fine," J.R. answered suspiciously. "Okay, what do you want?"

"Want? What makes you think I want something?"

"Maybe because you've been so uptight all night, this sudden change of mood, makes me, well, a little—"

Chris grabbed his heart and backed into the rack. "I'm hurt. It's just that I found my skis and I want to show them to you."

"Really? You found the K-2s."

"Well, not exactly, but close. They're my second choice, but they're perfect. There's only one snag."

"Snag?" J.R. cocked his head. "What kind of snag? Why don't you cut to the chase?"

Chris sighed. "All right, you've got me. Look, J.R., the skis really are perfect, it's just that I don't have enough money. How about a loan?"

"I would if I could, but I'm busted." He stuck his hands in his coat pocket and pulled out a handful of change and some fuzzy lint. "Unless a dollar thirty-two is all you're missing."

"Not quite," Chris said, and became glum again.

"I'd help you if I could, you know I would."

"I know. Sorry I was so sneaky about it. It's just that I want these skis so bad." Chris emphasized the point by slamming his hand on the end of the rack.

"Let's find the other guys and see if they'll chip in. Here, you can have my dollar thirty-two."

"I can't ask them. They have stuff they want to get, too. Everybody's been saving for this night. I just didn't save enough."

"Don't give up yet. I saw Stretch and Gadget over by the hats and gloves." J.R. grasped Chris's sleeve and pulled him to the tables. Stretch and Gadget saw them coming and looked up.

"Sorry, Chris, we already talked to Jack and we can't help you out, either," Stretch said.

"I'm trying to get these new boots—Nordicas. They're great but they'll be expensive, so I'm afraid I'm a little low on finances, too," Gadget said, displaying the boots he wanted to get.

Chris tried to smile. "Good choice. They look great."

"Well, your problem isn't solved, Chris," J.R. cried. "I say we tackle Jack and make him give us the extra cash."

"I can't do that," Chris said. "He's got things he wants to buy, too."

"Not really," J.R. grunted. "He's just being stingy."

"Hey, what about Alex?" Stretch suggested.

Chris perked up. "There's an idea. She should be loaded."

Stretch continued. "She's got all her tips from helping her dad out at the diner. A lot of it from us since we go in there so much. She should be grateful. If it weren't for us Mike's Diner might go under."

"I wouldn't go that far," Gadget said. "But it's worth a try."

J.R. nodded. "We can ask at least."

"Okay, Gadget and I will try to work our magic on Jack," Stretch instructed. "And the two of you put the pressure on Alex."

"Thanks, guys," Chris said. "I really appreciate your help. Let's meet back at the skis in fifteen minutes."

"Look," J.R. said, and pointed out Alex, who was by the ski clothes. "Let's get her before she decides to spend any of her dough." Chris and J.R. dashed across the gym. "You don't want that," J.R. cried as he tugged Alex's arm away from a neon-pink ski jacket.

Alex glared at J.R. "Why not? I think it's cool."

"That's the problem," Chris added, picking up on J.R.'s lead. "On the slopes you want to be warm, not cool."

Alex put her hands on her hips. "You want to feel warm, but look cool."

"Okay, well, yeah, but the color's all wrong," Chris continued.

"You're cracked," Alex snapped as she snatched the coat off the rack. "I look great in pink. What are you two up to?"

"Are we really that transparent?" Chris asked. "I knew I should have just leveled with you, but—"

"But what?" Alex asked, slipping the jacket on.

"Chris found the neatest skis and wants to bid on them, but he doesn't have enough money," J.R. blurted out.

Alex walked over to a mirror leaning against the wall and posed in front of it. "How do you know it's not enough?"

"Trust me," Chris groaned. "No one would sell them for fifty bucks. Please, Alex, it'd only be a loan, I'll pay you back as soon as I can."

"I don't know." Alex unzipped the top of her waist pack to get to her money. "I'm going to try to get this coat. I should have about fifteen dollars left over, I guess you can borrow it," she said, quickly counting the bills. "I won't even charge you interest for the first week."

"You're all heart." J.R. smirked.

Chris didn't wait for any more dickering. He took Alex's hand and shook it. "It's a deal. I'm indebted to you forever."

"You'd better not be," Alex said back. "I'll want the full amount by the end of the month."

"No problem." Chris cheered and jumped into the air. "I'm going to go put in my bid. I'll meet you by the skis. Let's hope I can squeeze the other ten out of Jack."

Chris hurriedly filled out a bid card and handed it to Mrs. Tye behind the auction table. Then he rushed back to protect his prize. Stretch, Jack, and Gadget were waiting for him.

"We were too late," Gadget said. "Jack had already picked out a hat, goggles, and some gloves."

"That's why I came tonight," Jack said, defending himself. "Quit making me feel guilty about spending my own money. Here's my last five bucks. Maybe if my skis or your stuff sells, you'll have enough."

"He can't wait that long," Gadget said. "But maybe the owner will take an IOU."

"I've got an idea," J.R. cried. He ran down the aisle, leaving the gang dumbfounded.

"Let's see these skis you want," Stretch said.

"Okay," Chris answered eagerly. "They're the best." He went to his secret hiding place and pulled the equipment out for everyone to see. "My new skis, ta-da."

"Your skis," Ron Porter called from the other end of the aisle. "What makes you think those are your skis?"

"I'm going to put in a bid, so it's only a matter of time," Chris said boldly.

"Dream on, Morton," Ron said, and snatched the skis out of Chris's hands. "Pretty good stuff."

"You're too late," Stretch stated. "These are going to be Chris's."

"I think not, bucko," Ron said, holding the skis tight to his chest.

"Don't be such a spoilsport," Gadget added.

"Or a jerk," Jack said, snatching the skis back.

Bursting in with a five-dollar bill clutched tightly in his fist, J.R. cried, "I got it."

For a moment the gang forgot about Ron Porter and congratulated J.R. "Way to go, J.R." Chris grinned from ear to ear. "Now it's a done deal."

"Where'd you get the money?" Jack asked.

"I sold my new gloves to a kid who's been eyeing them at school."

"What?" Stretch and Chris said together. "You shouldn't have done that."

"I wanted to help," J.R. said. "I can wear my old ones. It's okay, really."

"Now I feel terrible," Chris said.

"Not as bad as you're going to feel when you don't get those skis," Ron Porter added with his usual cockiness.

"Why don't you just go away and leave us alone, Porter. This has nothing to do with you." Chris was mad now.

"That's where you're wrong, Morton. You see, these are my skis, and I've just decided I don't want to sell them." He plucked the skis from Jack and walked toward the nearest exit.

Chapter 3

DO OR DIE

"Ron Porter is a creep," J. R. Klipp said after he slammed the old green wooden door that led into Mike's Diner.

Jack snarled. "He's worse than a creep."

"When will that guy get out of my life," Chris groaned, and the boys walked single file to their back booth. The restaurant was quiet at eight o'clock at night, and it seemed kind of tired and worn-out without the usual after-school bustle of activity.

"If I'd kept my mouth shut and just put my bid in, I'd have those skis now."

"I'm not so sure you would've wanted them if you'd known they were Porter's," Stretch argued.

"Why do you say that?" Chris asked.

"They'd be jinxed." Stretch said.

"He probably doesn't take care of his things," J.R. added.

"Yeah, you're better off without them," Jack agreed.

Chris couldn't hide his disappointment. "Thanks, guys, I know you're trying to cheer me up, but the fact is, I wanted those skis."

"I still don't know why your dad won't let you have new ones from his store," Stretch said.

"Yeah, tell him it'd be free advertising," J.R. suggested.

"I haven't tried that one," Chris said, trying to smile. "I'll give it a shot later."

Stretch picked up a menu. "Well, as long as we're here we might as well order."

"I can't believe you're still hungry after dinner and all those doughnuts and cider you downed," Chris murmured.

"Can I help if it I'm a growing boy?"

Jack snatched the menu from Stretch's hands. "Why are you looking at that? We already know what you're going to order."

"Oh, yeah."

"Yeah," Jack continued. "You'll have a jumbo hot dog, fries, and a Coke. J.R. will have his gross chili with cheese and onions. Gadget orders that stupid minestrone soup, tuna platter on rye, and an orange soda pop. I will have my usual cheeseburger and onion rings, and Chris will have grilled cheese, fries, and a strawberry malt."

"Not tonight," Chris said glumly.

"You're changing your order?" J.R. said, acting shocked.

"Nah, I'm just not very hungry. I think I'll pass on the food. I've still got to call my dad and ask him to

26

pick us up here." He slid out of the booth and walked toward the phone in the little alcove.

"Man, he's really bummed," Stretch said, watching Chris as he made his way to the phone.

"I wish there was something we could do," J.R. cried.

"He's a big kid," Jack continued. "He'll get over it or figure out something. He always does."

"Jack's right," Stretch agreed.

"Hey, I always am."

"I'll go up to the counter and tell Mike what we want," Gadget said. "He's going to want to close pretty soon."

"Don't look now, but Bad News Porter just walked in." Stretch pointed to the Raiders who were just bustling in the entrance.

"Oh, man, this is just what Chris needs," Stretch groaned.

"Forget Chris. That guy always makes me sick, too," J.R. added.

Jack moaned. "Not just him, his whole gang is rotten."

"Well, well, what do we have here?" Ron Porter grinned from ear to freckled ear as he strolled slowly to the back booth. "Look, guys, it's the sore losers."

Jack sat up straight. "Why don't you just get lost."

"Yeah, and never get found," Stretch added.

"Oh, you really scare me," dark-haired Greg Forbes said in a high soprano voice while he knocked his knees together.

"Maybe we want something to eat," Chubby Hank Thompson said.

"Yeah, I suppose you do need a little more padding, since you'll be falling all over the slopes," Jack said, primed for a fight.

"What's that supposed to mean?" Hank asked.

"Figure it out." Jack smirked and stuck his chin out.

"Look, I'll match my guys on the slopes against you wimps any day," Ron added.

"No sweat," Jack fired back.

"Besides how would you know how we ski?" Pete Farrell added, picking up a menu from the High-Fives' table.

"Yeah, you've never even gotten off the bunny hill." The Raiders laughed.

"Speaking from experience, Porter?" Chris asked as he and Gadget made their way back to the table.

Ron turned around. "Well, if it isn't the big loser."

"Actually, I'm very relieved. You did me a big favor. If I'd have known it was your equipment, I never would have bid on it. Why waste money on something that would fall apart the first time I hit a mogul."

"That equipment is first rate," Ron fired back, his face so red his freckles vanished.

"Then why were you selling it?" Chris elbowed his way past Randy and Ron to take his seat in the booth.

"Put up or shut up, Morton," Ron added. "I can outski you with only one ski on."

"Which is what you'll have to do on that flimsy equipment."

"Yeah, well, why were you dying to have it?"

"I thought it might be a challenge to fix it up, but now you've spared me the hassle," Chris added.

"I'll take you on any time you want, Morton," Ron said.

Chris didn't back down. "Fine with me."

"And since we're all going skiing, we'll be able to," Randy added, striking a macho pose with his feet wide apart and his arms crossed.

"You're on," Chris stated.

"You name the time and place," Ron challenged.

"And you be sure to be there," Chris finished. " 'Cause we'll be ready to wipe your faces in the snow."

Ron Porter laughed. "Don't count on it, High-Fives. Come on, guys, let's split." The Raiders zipped up their jackets and stomped out of Mike's.

"This has gone on long enough," Chris said, staring at the door the Raiders had just swaggered through. "This time we're going to shut them up for good."

Chapter 4

HITTING THE SLOPES

"Dad, it's really important to me. Please, please, can't I have some K-2s," Chris said, shadowing his dad around Morton's Sporting Goods Store the next day.

"Chris, I've gone over this several times already. I can't give you all the latest equipment every time you want to be involved in a new sport. If you recall, you have a skate board and a hockey stick collecting dust in your bedroom." Mr. Morton continued to stock the shelves.

"But this *is* different. I've been skiing for years. I'll never give it up."

"That's great, but as you know, ski equipment is very expensive. You did get new boots last season. Maybe in a few years when you've stopped growing, we can talk about new skis."

"What am I supposed to do this year?"

"Your old skis are still in great shape, Chris. Who

knows, you still may find some used equipment before the season's up."

"I tried to get some stuff, but it didn't work out."

"And I'm sorry, but that doesn't change the situation here."

"Why not?" Chris slumped against a baseball display.

"Chris . . ." Mr. Morton tried to be sympathetic.

But Chris wasn't ready to give up, and he continued to follow his dad like a lost puppy. "How about this. Have you ever thought about how much free advertising you'd get if I were decked out in all the best stuff. Kids would ask me where I got it, and then they'd come here and buy it from you."

Mr. Morton turned toward his son and smiled. "Nice try, Chris. You know your older brother Tim tried that line on me. But he didn't come up with it until he was in high school. Sandy tried it when she was interested in tennis."

"Sandy played tennis?"

"My point exactly. She never stuck with it so she has a very expensive racquet that would get better use as a spaghetti strainer."

"But you know I'm going to use the skis."

"Chris, this conversation is over. You have very nice Head XRs. Any seventh grader would love to own them. So quit asking me. I'll tell you the same thing I told Tim and Sandy—you get a twenty-five percent discount from the store. Now if you'd like, you can rent and try something new that way."

"But I don't want to rent, I want to own the K-2s."

"And I'd like to drive a Jaguar, but I can't afford it."

He stepped back behind the counter and filed the stock sheet. "I've got a lot of work to do, so we can't discuss this anymore."

"Bummer." Chris sighed, giving up—for then. "Are you still going to take us all over to the YMCA tomorrow morning?"

"You bet. Now remember, we have to leave the house at five A.M., so get to bed early. You don't want to fall asleep on the slopes, or worse, have an accident because you're tired."

"I know, Dad," Chris said. "See you later." Chris wandered slowly through the ski clothes before walking out into the crisp January air of Conrad. He stepped closer to the ski display in the front window. Three mannequins, dressed in top of the line Obermeyer clothes, were wearing replicas of gold Olympic medals. A sign read "Ski for the Prize." One figure held a pair of Karhu cross-country skis. Opposite that mannequin was a neon-clad snow boarder.

Stretch had talked about trying one of those surf boards for the snow, since they'd come out with the new and modified boards for kids. Chris figured he'd stick with the two-ski method. The third mannequin was posed on top of a mound of cotton and glitter and was racing to the finish line on Chris's dream K-2 skis. They were made for me, he thought. Slowly his expression changed from frustration to optimism. "I haven't given up yet," he said softly. "Before this season is over, that will be me skiing for the prize."

*   *   *

Early the next morning the ringing of the alarm clock sent chills through Chris. He bolted upright out of a dead sleep, groped for the snooze button, and then crashed back onto the bed and settled under the warm covers again. He had to blink his eyes several times before he could focus on the blurry digital read-out. "Four A.M.," he mumbled in a froggy voice. He'd had a hard time getting to sleep the night before, and now he regretted it. He'd promised himself he'd be asleep by nine P.M., but it hadn't worked out that way. He was too excited, and could only toss and turn thinking about the first Downhillers Club ski day. Did he have the right clothes? Should he have had his edges sharpened again? He'd tested his bindings to be sure he had a snug but safe fit. They had to be tight enough to take the shocks of all the moguls he'd be pounding, but not too tight so they wouldn't release if he had a bad fall.

Chris wasn't really afraid of having an accident, but he had to admit that it did cross his mind. "Not today," he said, throwing the covers back. He stood up and padded toward the bathroom at the end of the hall. The rest of the house was dark, since no one was up yet. Chris flicked on the light in the bathroom and squinted in the glare. His toes wrinkled up to escape the shock of cold tile. After a splash of water, he was ready to get dressed.

The first layer was his bright red long john bottoms. They were starting to creep up toward his calves, maybe he'd outgrow his Heads and get those K-2s before he knew it. He slipped on his polypropylene undershirt, which helped to keep him warm and dry no matter what the weather was. It drew moisture away from his skin as well as adding warmth. He slipped on his Thur-Lo padded socks next, then his bright blue turtleneck, and Thinsulate pants. He did a few squats to check out his flexibility. It was nice to have thin layers keeping him so warm. He pulled on his sneakers, leaving the laces undone, grabbed his red and yellow sweater, matching headband, Gates brand gloves, and lucky red bandanna scarf before bounding downstairs.

Mr. Morton had gotten up and was shuffling to the coffeepot. "Eat something before you go. It's a long trip and a big day."

"Right, Dad," Chris answered, the frog still croaking in his throat.

"Your mother packed you a lunch. It's in the refrigerator."

Chris rolled his eyes. It wasn't cool to brown-bag it, but he'd take it with him, buy lunch, and use his mom's lunch as a snack on the trip home. He was always hungry then. "Thanks, Dad."

"Don't thank me, thank your mother—she made the lunch. Did you stick your equipment in the van?"

"Last night," Chris said, pouring milk on his cereal.

Ten minutes later Chris and his dad pulled into the Evanses' driveway and loaded Stretch, his skis, boots, and poles into the van. Not long after, all the High-Fives were in the van heading for the Y and their first trip up to Winter Park.

"Let's see if we can get the last two rows of the bus," J.R. said excitedly. "That way we'll be able to sit together. The last row has three seats and the one in front of it has two."

"Sounds good to me," Gadget said.

The parking lot of the Y looked like the first day of summer camp. Kids scampered around and parents stomped their feet against the cold. All of them were lugging skis with poles dangling off in all directions. Chris was kind of glad when his dad finally left and it was just the guys starting off on a new High-Fives adventure. They stowed their skies and poles in the storage compartment under the bus and were anxious to leave.

"Bad news," Stretch said, coming out of the bus. "It looks like a group of girls had the same idea as J.R.— the backseats are already taken."

"I saved us three rows in the middle," Gadget said.

"Great, let's go for it," Jack added. "I've got dibs on a window seat."

"Only if I don't beat you to it," Chris shouted, taking off. The gang bounded up the metal steps and threw their jackets onto the overhead metal racks. "This is going to be great," Chris said. He settled into his window seat, happy because the Raiders weren't on their bus.

"Hey, look," Stretch said. "The seats go back." He pushed a button on the armrest and the dark blue cushion reclined into the lap of the passenger behind him.

"I hope you're not planning to ride like that all the way to Winter Park," Alex said sarcastically.

"And good morning to you, too," Stretch replied.

"Hi, Alex," J.R. cried from his seat two rows ahead.

"I hope we get moving soon," Gadget groaned. The smell of diesel fuel is making me sick." Moments later the bus driver closed the door, shifted into gear, and the Downhillers Club was on the road. "All right!" the entire busload of kids shouted. The kids were too busy laughing and talking, so hardly anyone noticed the sun rising over the mountains, the early-morning traffic, or the light snowfall that was making small mounds on top of the evergreens during the two-and-a-half-hour trip up to Winter Park. Before pulling into the parking lot the kids could see the manicured slopes and chair lifts that dotted the mountainside. The High-Fives piled out of the bus, gathered up their equipment, and got their tow tickets from Mrs. Tye, who was chaperoning for the club.

"Head 'em up and move 'em out," Alex called to the others.

"Last one up to the top is a rotten egg," Chris added.

"Hold on, guys, I'm starved. I've got to get something to eat before we start." Jack set his skis and poles in the rack and pointed to the warming house a few yards away.

"Didn't you eat before you left?" Chris asked, unable to hide his disappointment.

"Who can eat at four-thirty in the morning?" Jack answered.

"I can," Chris muttered under his breath.

"Where's Stretch?" J.R. asked, looking around.

"I think he's still on the bus, sound asleep," Gadget replied, leaning against the side of the bus.

"Asleep," Chris cried. "What's he sleeping for?"

"Maybe he's tired," Jack answered.

"We didn't come to Winter Park to sleep," Chris said.

J.R. stepped back on the bus. "I'll see if I can wake him up."

"I don't feel very good," Gadget grumbled, still against the bus. "I didn't think a bus could make me carsick. Why don't you guys go on without me, I'll catch up with you around lunch."

"I don't believe this," Chris said, flinging his arms up into the air in frustration. "We came here to ski."

"Well, you'd better count Stretch out, he's zonked," J.R. said as he returned to the group.

"You've got to be kidding." Chris whirled around and kicked a clump of snow with the toe of his boot. "Stretch is sleeping, Jack's going to eat, and Gadget's sick. I guess J.R. and I will have to go to the top without you guys."

"W-well," J.R. stammered. "To be perfectly honest, I'm not sure I'm ready to go up to the top yet."

"What?" Chris screamed. "I can't believe you guys. A week ago you were all bragging about what hotshots you were, and now I can't even get you to put on your skis."

"Take it easy, Morton," Jack said. "We're going to be skiing later."

"But the best snow is always in the morning."

Jack tried to calm Chris down. "And you'll ski it."

"This is crazy," Chris said, still frustrated.

"Look, I'll go grab a quick bite to eat. The cold air should revive Gadget, Stretch will wake up any minute, and you can give J.R. some pointers," Jack said. "Besides, the lines to the top are pretty long right now."

Chris crossed his arms over his chest. "I guess I don't have any choice unless I want to ski alone, or try to catch up with Alex and her girlfriends."

"Come on, you can coach me. It won't be so bad." J.R. tried to sound positive.

"Sounds good to me," Gadget added.

"All right, I'll meet you back here in half an hour."

"Better make it an hour and a half," Jack said, unbuckling the top two buckles on his boots. "I don't know how long the lines in the cafeteria will be."

"That long, no way. Look, my mom packed me a lunch, why don't you eat it and then you won't have to wait in line."

"Thanks, but no thanks," Jack said, moving toward the warming house. "I don't want lunch, I need breakfast."

"I give up," Chris said, grabbing his skis. "Come on, J.R., we'll work on some fundamentals over on the ski-school hill."

"Great," J.R. answered, obviously feeling more secure.

"I'll bet Porter and his Raiders don't have my problems." Chris studied the Iron Horse chair lift and sighed. He wished he were on it going up to a group of runs rather than making his way to the ski-school learner's hill.

"Thanks for working with me," J.R. said with a smile.

"No problem," Chris said, and returned his grin.

"You know they have a good ski school here if you want to take a lesson."

"I've taken lessons. I'm just a little nervous my first time up this season."

"Hey, I'm a little nervous every time, don't worry about it. Get your skis on and let's go." A few minutes later Chris added, "We'll start by doing a herringbone up the hill."

"Herringbone?"

"Plant your poles on the outsides of your skis, and place your skis in a *V* shape. Use your inside edges to dig into the snow, and step up the hill."

"This feels weird," J.R. said, puffing up the gentle slope. "But it works. They taught us the sidestep in my class."

"Either way and you'll get to the top." Chris hopped around on his skis trying to get a feel for the snow. "Now, how far did you get in your class?"

J.R. scratched at his head through his wool hat. "Stem turns and stem christies—I think that's what they called them."

Chris pointed down the hill below them. "Okay, let's see how much you remember."

J.R. angled himself to cut across the slope rather than straight down it. Using his edges to keep himself in place, he pushed off gently, his knees slightly bent and his weight forward to propel him along. After traversing a few feet across the slope, he bent his knees farther, shifted all of his weight to his downhill ski, lifted his uphill ski, and moving the tips together, aimed downhill for an instant before sliding the skis together. He had turned and was gliding across the hill in the other direction now.

"Perfect," Chris cheered. "You're a natural."

"Perfect, ha!" a voice yelled from the chair lift line a few yards away.

Chris craned his neck to see who had made the comment. It was Ron Porter. He and the rest of the Raiders were about to head up on the lift. "Ignore him," Chris called.

"Make sure you don't fall down," Randy Salazar whined.

"You might get a boo-boo," Peter Farrell added.

"Bunny hill or bust," Ron Porter called out as he plopped into the chair to take him to the top of the mountain.

Chris lowered his head, embarrassed. "I'd like to bust you instead, Porter," he whispered to himself.

Chapter 5

THE FIRST RUN

"Stretch, wake up," Chris said, shaking his friend, who was still sound asleep on the bus. He'd finished helping J.R., taken off his skis, and was back at the bus after an hour and a half.

"I've never seen anybody sleep so soundly," J.R. said, peering down at Stretch.

"Maybe this is why he has so much energy during the day," Gadget added.

Chris slumped into the seat in the row opposite Stretch. "I don't believe this."

"Should we wake him up?" Jack whispered.

"I don't care," Chris said. "I'm going skiing in fifteen minutes with or without him, or without any of you."

"Wake up, Stretch," J.R. said, leaning into Stretch's face.

"Hey, Evans, snap out of it," Jack practically shouted.

Gadget nudged him gently. "Stretch, it's time to go skiing."

"Huh, what's happening?" Stretch grumbled, still curled up.

"You're asleep on the ski bus," Jack moaned, giving Stretch a shove. "What a sleepyhead."

"Just five more minutes, Mom," Stretch murmured.

"Mom," Jack said, jumping back. "Who are you calling Mom? This has gone on long enough." Jack grabbed Stretch by the shoulders and started to jostle him.

"Jack, what are you doing here?" Stretch said, opening first one eye and then the other.

"What am *I* doing here? *You* fell asleep on the ski bus, doofus." Jack stood up. "Come on, Chris, I'm with you. We've waited long enough. Let's hit the slopes."

"Finally," Chris cried. He looked at his watch. "At least we'll get a few hours of skiing in."

"I'm ready to go now, too." Gadget zipped up his jacket.

"Me, too," J.R. added.

"Well, don't forget me." Stretch rubbed his eyes and sat up.

"Do you always sleep this much?" J.R. asked.

"Well, sometimes," Stretch answered. "I couldn't get to sleep last night, so I stayed up and watched the midnight movie. I guess it wasn't a good idea."

"Especially with an altitude change. Theoretically you can go without sleep for a while, but eventually you do have to rest," Gadget rattled on. "And children should sleep longer than adults because their muscles and bones aren't fully developed."

"Well, my muscles and bones are ready to go skiing." Chris pulled on his hat and headed for the door. The others followed.

"Hey, look," Jack said, pointing to the lift line. "It's practically empty, we'll be on the top in no time."

For the first time in hours, Chris was happy and relaxed. He helped J.R. with his skis and then after putting on his own, glided to the lift line. "High-Fives, ho."

"I'll go up alone," Jack said, offering to ride by himself while the others paired up for the two-seater lift.

"Hey look, there's Alex. Maybe she'd like to go with us," Gadget said, waving his mittened hand. "Alex, come and join us."

"Be right there," Alex called, waving a pole in the air.

"I'm not riding up with her." Jack sidestepped out of line.

"I will," Gadget volunteered, waving his arm again.

"Yeah, but you were paired up with J.R., and it'll be even worse to ride with him," Jack said directly in his brother's face.

"Oh, for heaven's sake," Chris groaned. "I'll ride with J.R., and you can go with sleeping beauty here. Let's just get going."

The gang rearranged their order and then glided along the ruts in the snow that led to the chair lift. They slipped their poles off their wrists and "skated" closer to the chair. Chris and J.R. were first.

"Hello there," the tow operator said cheerfully. She checked their tickets. "You picked a great day to ski." The chair lift was designed with the armrest on the outside, so the boys stood side by side with their backs to the chairs, their poles in the inside hands.

"Here it comes," Chris said, glancing back. "You ready?"

J.R. nodded. "Ready as I'll ever be." The chair swung noisily through the last gate while Chris and J.R. peered over their outside shoulders. They clutched the bar as the attendant slowed the chair down, and then with a *whoosh*, the boys felt themselves being seated and lifted into the air, their skis dangling below them.

"All right," Chris cheered. "Meet you guys at the top," he added, turning back to the others still at the gate.

"Sure is pretty," J.R. said, staring out over the horizon.

"Yeah, you can see for miles." Snow-capped mountains surrounded them on three sides. The clear sky and sunshine made it a perfect day to ski. It was cold enough to keep the snow in good shape, but warm enough to make the ride on the chair comfortable. On cold or windy days the lift ride could get awfully chilly. "You excited to take your first run of the season?" Chris asked, smiling at J.R.

"I guess so," J.R. answered.

Chris swung his skis gently. They were nice skis, he thought. Not what he'd hoped to be wearing, but the bindings were good, and as his dad had said, they were better than what most kids his age had. *"Tee yodel ode lay he hoo,"* Chris yodeled into the air. It wasn't a real yodel, but it sounded good.

"Teach me to do that," J.R. pleaded.

"Just bounce your tongue around in your throat."

J.R. gave it a shot, but it sounded wrong.

"Hey, when did they let sick cows on the slopes?" Stretch called from the chair behind.

"Very funny," J.R. replied over his shoulder.

The rest of the ride Chris watched the skiers, schussing on the slopes below them in smooth rhythmic hops. As they approached the last few tow poles that held the lift in the air, they prepared to unload. The boys put their ski tips up slightly, scooted forward in their seats, and waited for the chair to nudge them onto the platform and down the gentle slope to the top of the runs. "Let's wait for the others by the map," Chris said, skating off. He was confident on skis, and did a hockey stop, spraying the loose top snow into a feathery plume. Chris bent down and tightened the top buckles of his boots. Sometimes it cut off his circulation if he left them buckled for the lift ride. J.R. and Chris had slipped their hands through the wrist straps of their poles and were grasping the tops as they waited for the others.

"Which run should we take first?" Stretch asked, checking his bindings. "Cheshire cat or Jabberwocky?"

"Aren't those both intermediate runs?" J.R. said, a little nervously.

Jack slipped on his pole straps. "What of it?"

"I hoped we'd start out a little slower," J.R. whispered.

"I wouldn't mind getting the bugs out on a beginner slope, too," Gadget said, unfogging his glasses.

Stretch tightened the strap on his Carrera goggles. "I don't want to spend the whole day on the beginner slopes."

"No, you'd rather sleep," Chris added. The others laughed.

"Actually, Allan Phipps is pretty clear right now," Alex said, pointing out one of the easier slopes.

Jack stomped his skis in the snow. "Well, all right, but I'm not taking Mock Turtle no matter how much you beg."

"Look, we could all use a practice run," Chris said, making the final decision. "We'll start on Allan Phipps and work up to Engledive by the end of the day."

"Isn't that a black slope?" J.R. asked.

"Sounds good to me," Stretch said as he pushed off.

"I don't think I'll do any advanced slopes," J.R. added.

"Then don't," Jack said. He pushed off first by bending his knees and setting his skis in a parallel position to the slope.

Gadget flipped open his trail map. "Let's make our way over to the Looking Glass lift. There are lots of green marked beginner runs, or blue marked intermediate slopes. That should make everyone happy."

"Tally-ho," Alex called, ready for action. "We can take Butch's Breezeway then, that's my favorite."

The gang started out single file and looked as if they were playing follow the leader. Chris loved the way the snow squeaked under his skis. He smoothly traversed, crossing back and forth on the open part of the slope, plotting his course. He found himself humming a tune, and laughed. Humming always helped him keep a smooth, steady rhythm.

Chris led, followed by Jack, Stretch, J.R., Alex, and Gadget. Before long they'd made it to the crest of the hill that led to the widest part of the slope.

"Now this is living," Chris panted, trying to catch his breath.

"Yeah, it doesn't get any better than this," Stretch added.

"Alex was right, we practically have the hill to ourselves." Gadget snow-plowed to a smooth stop.

"How's it feel?" Chris said to J.R.

"Great," J.R. answered. "I had a good coach this morning."

"Then let's keep moving." Stretch took the lead, and the others followed in formation.

Chris decided to test out his ankle strength, and pointed his skis down the fall line, an imaginary line that follows the straightest path down any slope. Using his poles he gently parallelled down a giant slalom course he created in his mind. After twenty feet, he hit an icy patch, his edges loosened their grip, and he toppled over as if he'd slipped on a huge banana peel. His left ski tip was the first to go, crossing over his right ski. He tumbled forward and landed hard on his shoulder. He felt a freezing sensation up his back as he slid a few yards before stopping with his face down in the snow. "Uh," Chris groaned, and tried to take an instant physical inventory. He'd be all right.

47

"You okay,?" Alex asked. She was the first to get to him.

"I think so," Chris grumbled. He sat up and slid his goggles up on his forehead. "I hit some ice."

"What a cool wipe-out," Stretch said, sidestepping closer to Chris. "You're all right, aren't you?"

"Yeah, but, boy, is this snow cold." Chris shook the back of his jacket and a mound of snow tumbled back onto the slope.

"Well, I guess you buy the first round of hot chocolate," Jack said from a few feet away.

"Right, I forgot. The first one to fall buys the hot stuff." Chris looked around him. "Anyone seen my right ski?"

"I got it," J.R. called out from above the gang.

"It's nice to know my equipment works."

"Yep," J.R. said, handing Chris his ski. "Your safety prongs dug right into the snow."

"Here, let me give you a hand," Gadget said.

Chris sat sideways and, using his poles on the downhill side, pushed himself to a standing position. He tapped the caked snow off the bottom of his boots and stepped into his bindings. With a pop, he was ready to go again.

"What do we have here?" Ron Porter's voice came from above.

Chris raised his head to see Ron and Greg riding on the chair lift just above them. "Not now," Chris grumbled.

"Hey, Morton, maybe you'd better go back to the

bunny hill. If you fall there, though, you'd better think about taking up sledding.'' Ron continued jeering, and Chris and the other High-Fives could do nothing but listen to the laughter as it bounced and echoed off the mountains. This wasn't exactly what Chris had dreamed his first ski day with the Downhillers would be like.

Chapter 6

MEETING THE CHALLENGE

"Okay, we've skied down that beginner's slope Mock Turtle three times. I think J.R.'s ready to advance to the big blues." Chris's voice had an edge to it since his run-in with Ron Porter.

"The big blues?" J.R. asked.

"All the slopes have symbol and color guides to help skiers ski within their limits," Gadget explained. "Greens circles are for beginners. Blues squares are for intermediates. But a blue square with a black diamond designates a more difficult slope. A black diamond by itself marks the most difficult, expert slopes."

"Chris is trying to say that you've done really well this afternoon, and you're ready to advance to the intermediate slopes, the ones marked by a blue square." Stretch gave J.R.'s shoulder a pat.

"You really think so," J.R. said with a smile.

"Definitely," Stretch said, and tossed a snowball at J.R.

Jack shuffled his skis forward and backward as the gang gathered beside the small warming house at the base of the Looking Glass and Olympia lifts. "I'm glad because I wouldn't take another practice run on Mock Turtle. I said I wouldn't do it all."

"You're just sore 'cause you wiped out on it," Stretch teased.

"I did not wipe out, I was getting out of the way of that wacko beginner, and just sort of sat down," Jack explained quickly.

"Sure," J.R. razzed. "Anyway, I think I'm ready."

"Great, then it's time to give Butch's Breezeway a shot," Alex suggested. The gang pushed off from the small warming station and glided toward the lift.

"You're a pretty good skier," Chris said to Alex as they rode the chair lift together. "Have you been skiing a long time?"

"A few years. I like it a lot, but I'm afraid I go a little nuts skiing with some of my girlfriends. They want to stop after every run to fix their hair and stuff."

"Doesn't it just get messed up again?"

"Yeah. I'd rather get in more ski time."

"Me, too."

"You know you shouldn't let Porter get to you."

"What?" Chris said, surprised. "He doesn't get to me."

"Sure. Then why have you been crabby all afternoon?"

"That's not it." Chris was thinking back to all the

51

hassles they'd had getting on the slopes and all the time they'd wasted. "You're probably right, he does bug me too much. He's always around at the wrong time. That is, if there's any good time for him to be around."

"I admit he's a creep, but he knows he can get to you, and the other guys, too, so he keeps doing it." Alex slipped her poles under her outside thigh, so she wouldn't have to hold them for the ride. "You might try ignoring him. That'll drive him crazy."

"Hey, maybe he'll fall into a snow drift and we'll be done with him once and for all."

Alex prepared to unload. "Don't count on it."

Chris skied to a big sign that directed skiers to various slopes. "Think J.R.'s ready to take Engledive?" he teased.

Alex stared at the black diamond shape next to the name indicating that it was an expert slope. "Are you?"

"We're taking Butch's, right?" Stretch asked, gliding up.

"Yep," Chris said cheerfully.

"Let's do it then," Jack added.

"I'm ready," J.R. said.

"Look who's getting off the lift." Gadget nodded to the Raiders, who were unloading and heading their way.

"Let's split," Chris said, slipping his hands into his pole straps.

"I'm with you," Alex said, remembering their conversation.

"Let's take it easy, and have fun," Chris added.

"What do we have here?" Ron said, schussing up to the crowd.

"You guys taking Mock Turtle?" Greg Forbes joked.

"No, jerk face," Jack answered.

"We're going down Engledive," Randy Salazar said. "Want to join us?"

"What do you think, guys?" Chris asked, taking in all the High-Fives and Alex.

"Fine with me," Jack said defiantly.

"Uh, I don't know," Gadget said, peering down at the steep hill covered with moguls.

"Too much for you, brain boy?" Hank asked.

"You can do it, Gadget," Stretch said.

"Then let's go." Peter Farrell turned toward the slope.

"I challenge you, Morton," Ron said with a sneer.

Chris shrugged his shoulders. "To what?"

"A race, what else? My Raiders against your High-Fives."

"What's that going to prove?" Alex questioned.

"No one asked you, Alex, but it'll prove who's the best skier, that's what."

'We don't have to prove anything." Stretch grinned. "We know we're good."

"Then put up or shut up," Ron added quickly.

"You're on," Chris said confidently.

"Okay, first group to have everyone down at the bottom—with their skis on—wins."

J.R. looked at the slope and felt his throat drop into his stomach.

Chris noticed him and decided to take back the challenge. "On second thought, I don't think I want to."

"Chicken," Greg snapped.

"I'm not chicken, I just don't want to waste my time."

The other High-Fives acted stunned. "Come on, Chris, it might be worth a couple of laughs," Stretch cried.

"You can say that again." Porter chuckled. "We'll be laughing at you guys tumbling all the way down."

Chris glanced at J.R. again. He knew J.R. wouldn't be able to take the run. And even if he tried, it wouldn't be a smart move, especially now that his confidence was just beginning to grow. "Nah, I think we'll stick to our original game plan."

Ron leaned his chin on the handles of his poles. "Maybe it's because your equipment isn't good enough."

Chris's blood started to boil. "It has nothing to do with my equipment. We just don't want to, right, guys?"

The High-Fives were all silent.

"Come on, Chris," Jack whispered. "We can take them."

"We don't have to," Chris said back quietly.

"Put up, or shut up," Ron repeated.

Chris shifted his aim toward Butch's Breezeway. "Come on, guys, we're wasting precious ski time."

"So it's Engledive, right?" Stretch said.

"No, we're doing Butch's."

"But, Chris—" Jack muttered.

"I'll try," J.R. said meekly.

"No, you won't," Chris stated.

"I can do it." J.R. tried to sound confident.

Chris planted his poles in the snow. "Okay, Porter, you want a challenge, let's do it, just you and me. First man down wins."

"You got it," Porter said, grinning from ear to ear.

"Don't do it for me," J.R. said.

"I'm not," Chris said back. "I'm doing it for me." He avoided Alex's glance. He couldn't ignore Porter, not that day anyway.

"Then let's do it," Porter added.

"What about the rest of us?" Randy Salazar asked.

"I'll take you on," Jack answered.

"What about you, four eyes?" Hank said to Gadget.

"I'll pass," Gadget said frankly. "I said I was going to ski Butch's Breezeway with my friends and that's exactly what I plan to do."

"Chicken," Hank said under his breath.

"What about you, Evans?" Greg asked.

Stretch was almost happy. "Sounds like fun to me. What does the winner get?"

"He doesn't get humiliated," Ron said.

Chris tried to gain control. "Jack, Stretch, this is between Porter and me. Why don't you go with the others and we'll meet at Snoasis for something to drink."

"Don't tell me what to do," Jack snapped. "If I want to race Salazar, I will."

"I didn't mean that," Chris said, apologizing.

"Well, I think the whole thing sounds like a bunch of macho bragging." Alex shook her head. "Come on, J.R. and Gadget."

Chris sidestepped closer to Stretch and Jack. "Please, you guys, let's not make a big deal out of this. Besides,

I need you to be at the bottom to see who wins. I don't trust Porter, he could try to pull something funny."

"I've got an idea," Jack said. "I'll ski partway down and watch from there, and Stretch, you go down to the finish line."

"Perfect," Chris said, smiling.

"Jack and I think it's more important to work as officials on this challenge," Stretch said, before starting down the slope.

"Are you saying that I'd cheat," Porter said, scrunching up his nose.

"Bingo," Jack said, as he pushed off his poles and started down Engledive to his post midway.

"Let's go ski Butch's," Alex said to J.R. and Gadget.

"No, I want to watch this," Gadget said.

"Okay," Alex said. "But we can watch from the bottom where Butch's and Engledive merge. If we go now we can see the whole silly thing."

Chris took a deep breath. "Okay, what are the rules?"

"Rules." Ron laughed. "There are no rules. First one to the bottom with his skis on wins."

"Fine," Chris added.

"So if you ride in a toboggan, it doesn't count," Greg said.

"Very funny," Chris said. "Let's get to it as soon as everyone's in position at the bottom."

"Ready when you are." Ron watched the others reach the bottom and then got into a low crouch.

Chris had been studying the narrow, steep hill and now he plotted his path. Suddenly his legs felt stiff and awkward. He wished he'd taken a tougher run that morning instead of all those beginner's slopes with the High-Fives. I should have had some lunch, too, he thought.

Randy raised his blue bandanna scarf. "Racers ready?"

"Ready," Ron boomed.

"Ready," Chris echoed.

"On your marks, get set, and"—Randy paused—"and go."

Chris pushed off with all his might. He bent his knees harder than he'd done that morning, and tucked his poles under his arms. The first few yards felt good. His edges met the loose top snow, and his first easy turn took him to a series of moguls. Chris's skis bounced unsteadily so he widened his stance to support the blows. Keep your skis together, he reminded himself, you'll lose time in you don't. Chris sat back into the gully between the next few bumps, shooting his skis forward with each effort. With a grunt, and another turn, he raced into an open flat spot.

"Push it, Chris." Jack's voice rang out in encouragement a few yards down.

Chris caught a glimpse of Ron out of the corner of his eye. They were almost even, but Ron did have a slight advantage.

"Attack the hill, attack," Chris murmured under his breath. He planted his pole ahead of his right ski, and with a quick shift of his weight, and a bounce of his ankles, he gained on Ron. You've got him now, he thought, but Ron was still ahead.

Then suddenly, as Chris started to bound over the next set of moguls, they swallowed him like waves. The harder he tried, the more control he lost. He flung his arms out to regain his balance. The distance between his skis widened and his edges were soft, unable to grip the hill. His rhythm got off, and he lurched forward, getting sucked into the gully between two moguls. To combat the forward motion, he sat back too far. The tails of his skis scooted forward and he fell back—hard. "Uh," he groaned, trying to struggle to his feet and continue the race. With his skis still in the air, Chris rolled to his side and for a moment regained control and was on his feet, but before he could get totally back on line, he was down and tumbling fast. A mouthful of snow and a few minutes later he stopped between two bumps and watched Ron slide past him to win.

"Darn." Chris slammed his fist into the snow. He lay there for a second letting the cold reality and the cold snow set in. "Why did I have to fall?"

"You okay?" Jack asked, skiing down to him.

"Yeah, sure," Chris said, hitting the snow again. "My pride is the only thing really hurt." He sat up and watched the Raiders crowd around Ron and cheer his success. "I let the gang down."

"Don't worry about it. We'll get them next time," Jack said, offering his hand.

Chris took a quick inventory of his body and equipment. Everything was still intact. As he had said, the only thing really bruised was his ego. "Yeah, next time." Alex had been right. If he'd just ignored Ron, he wouldn't have to face this humiliation.

58

"We'll get a rematch," Jack said positively.

Chris stared down at the end of the run again. The High-Fives were standing quietly, and Chris knew he'd let them down, big-time. "Let's get out of here." He moved his skis below his body and again using his poles pushed himself to his feet.

The very bottom of the slope was fast, but easy, or at least easier, Chris thought to himself. His legs were shaky and he felt unconfident. I should have hummed, he thought to himself again. If I would have hummed, I would've kept my rhythm, my control.

Ron was waiting for him. "Maybe you should go back to Allan Phipps, or better yet the bunny slope." Ron was loving every minute of his victory. "It could be that your equipment is lousy, but I doubt it." He laughed loudly and the other Raiders joined in. "Catch you losers later." He pushed off and skated through the snow. The Raiders followed like shadows.

"Tough luck," Stretch said, and threw an arm over Chris's shoulders.

"You looked great to me," J.R. added.

Chris glanced at him.

"U-until the fall that is," J.R. stammered.

"You must have hit some ice," Stretch said.

"Or a rocky patch," Gadget added.

Jack patted his buddy on the back. "Yeah, you took the hardest part of the slope."

"I couldn't have done it." J.R. tried to sound cheery.

Chris knew they all were lying. They just didn't know what else to say, but then neither did he, other than "sorry." Chris didn't say a word—he only stared at the snow glistening in the afternoon sun. Sorry, guys, he thought to himself, but couldn't get the words out.

"Let's take a break," Gadget suggested. "I'm cold and hungry."

"Me, too," Alex added.

Chris couldn't look at them then or on the bus ride home.

Chapter 7

THE RIGHT STUFF

"Dad, how much would it cost to rent some K-2 skis for this weekend?" Chris pushed himself up onto the carpeted counter where his dad did fittings for the rental equipment.

Mr. Morton smiled and flipped open his scratch pad. "I think fifteen dollars should do it. That would include bindings and poles."

"Really, Dad? That'd be great."

"I'm not always the enemy, you know." Mr. Morton went back to the racks, and pulled out Chris's dream skis.

"Hey, what are my boots doing in the bindings?"

"Well, I thought I might try to make you smile at least once this week. You've been moping around ever since you got back from Winter Park. Didn't you have a good time?"

"I guess so. I got off to kind of a rough start, but I'm determined to make next weekend the best ever. And these skis are going to help a lot. Thanks, Dad."

"Sure, but remember skis aren't the answer to all your problems."

"I know, but they'll make me feel better."

"You could try to talk to your mother or me if you want. We might be able to help."

"I know, but I think I want to go solo on this one."

"Okay." He slapped the toe of Chris's boot. "Step in and we'll get you ready for tomorrow."

Chris tossed and turned all night, replaying his fall on Engledive over and over. He couldn't get the disappointed faces of the High-Fives out of his mind. First he'd see them looking down at the snow, and then he'd remember the Raiders howling with laughter. He'd do about anything to wipe the smirks off their faces once and for all. Now with K-2's he'd have a shot at doing it.

"Okay, is everyone ready?" Stretch asked at the bus the next day.

"Yep," Jack answered. "I ate the biggest breakfast known to man this morning."

"I took some Dramamine, so the bus won't give me motion sickness, and I even brought one of my dad's surgical masks to keep from breathing the fumes." Gadget pulled the small white rectangle out of his pocket. "I'll be ready to hit the slopes as soon as the bus stops in the parking lot."

"Great," Stretch said. "And you'll all be relieved to know that I didn't stay up and watch a late movie. As a matter of fact, I went to bed at nine, so I'm ready to go."

"J.R., what about you?" Gadget asked.

J.R. beamed. "I've been practicing everything Chris taught me in the backyard, in the basement, and in my room. I feel like I could beat anyone this week."

"Actually the kid looks pretty good," Jack said. "I can vouch for his practicing. He drove Mom crazy pretending to be schussing through the laundry in the basement. He may make a pretty good skier after all."

"Whoa, I can hardly believe my ears. Jack Klipp actually gave his brother a compliment." Stretch leaned up against their bus pretending he was about to faint.

"Did Chris suspect anything when you told him we'd meet him here instead of having his dad pick us all up?"

"Not really, I explained that my dad was going out of town and wanted to drop me off. You guys were all on our way so we saved his dad the extra stops."

"So we're all set then," Jack said. "Whatever Chris wants today, let's be up for it."

"And that includes a run down Engledive," Stretch added.

"Hey, I'm ready," J.R. cried. "I may not ski down it like an expert, but I won't fall either."

Stretch gave J.R. the thumbs-up sign. "That's the ticket."

Gadget's voice dropped to a whisper. "What are we going to do if we run into the Raiders? They were rough on him all week."

"Well, I've made sure we're not on the same bus again. That's a start," Jack stated.

Gadget sighed. "All for one and one for all."

J.R. smiled. "Yep, the High-Fives' motto."

"Gee, this is like a High-Fives meeting without the president," Gadget added.

"Kind of creepy," Stretch continued.

"Not really," Gadget said. "I think it means the High-Fives are stronger than ever."

"Yeah, now let's watch for Chris and get ready to have the best day ever on the slopes." Stretch held his right hand up, and the others joined in a group high-five.

"Hey, what's going on," Chris asked as he walked up to the group. "It looks like I'm being impeached."

"Quite the opposite, my friend," Stretch said, looping an arm around Chris's shoulders. "We're just psyched for a day on the slopes, led, of course, by our fearless leader."

"Put your skis on our bus, Mr. president. We've saved the last row for us today."

"Really? Great."

"This is going to be the best day of skiing we've ever had."

Chris gently placed his rental skis on top of the pile in the luggage compartment. He'd borrowed his brother Tim's ski cover, so they wouldn't get scratched or nicked. He would surprise the gang with his secret weapon when they unloaded at Winter Park. The group piled into the bus, and Chris was relieved that everyone was so up. It helped him to forget the weekend before. He breathed a big sigh of relief and climbed up the stairs of the bus.

J.R. was standing on the last seat of the bus. "On top of ol' Smokey, all covered with snow."

"Can it, Klipp," a kid from Chris's class yelled, and threw an orange at J.R.

For a moment Chris thought it had to be one of the Raiders but he relaxed when he remembered they were on a different bus.

"What's in the bag?" Stretch asked Chris as the High-Fives and the other members of the Downhillers Ski Club unloaded their gear in the Winter Park parking lot.

"A secret," Chris answered with a grin.

"I'm going to get a bite to eat," Jack said, pulling his poles out of the bus.

"Oh, no, not again," Chris groaned. The others glared, too.

"Just kidding," Jack replied.

Chris picked up a handful of snow and pelted Jack. "Don't you even dare think about pulling that one again."

"Let's get our skis on and go," Stretch cheered.

Chris cheerfully unzipped his prize package. *"Voilà,"* he said, revealing the K-2's.

"Wow, when did you get those?" Jack asked.

"My dad's letting me rent them," Chris said.

Gadget held one ski up to admire it. "These are really nice."

"Can I try them out sometime today?" Jack asked.

Chris held the skis. "Sorry, pal, they're not leaving my feet."

"I bet you'd cream Porter on Engledive if you had these on."

Everyone glared at J.R.

"Maybe," Chris said, easing the tension. "Maybe."

"Well, I don't think we'll have to deal with Porter," J.R. cried. "I heard him say they were spending the day over at the Mary Jane ski area."

"Well then, let's stay at the Winter Park area and avoid those jokers altogether." Jack rubbed his gloved hands together.

"Sounds good to me," Chris said.

"Well, are we going skiing or what?" Stretch interrupted. "The lines are starting to build up and we haven't even gotten our lift tickets yet."

Everyone hustled to get organized, and within fifteen minutes the High-Fives were on the chair lift to the top.

"Which run is first?" Gadget asked, slipping his hands into his poles.

"How about if each of us picks a run?" Chris suggested.

"Yeah, now that's democracy in action," Gadget added. "You choose first, Chris."

Chris thought for a moment. "I say we do Allan Phipps."

"Really?" Jack asked, surprised.

"Yeah, just because I fell there, I can't let that run haunt me. Besides it's a good one to start on. Loosen us up for some of the harder hills."

"Great. Let's go." J.R. pushed off to lead the gang.

The group jumped into action and headed for the crest of the run. Chris could already feel the difference his new skis made. He felt more connected because his boots hugged the skis, and the skis felt at one with the light powdery snow.

"Hey, I've got a game for us to try," Stretch said. "The human slalom course."

"What's that?" J.R. asked.

"Okay, listen up. We space ourselves about twenty feet apart, down the slope. The guy on top is the first to go. He skis around everyone as if he was a slalom gate. You know, around the right on the first guy, the left on the second. After he passes the first couple of guys, the next guy starts the course. When you finish the last guy, you position yourself twenty feet away and we can do it all the way down the hill."

"Cool," Chris said.

"Sounds fun. You lead off, Stretch." Jack side-stepped until he was facing the fall line. "I'll be the bottom guy."

"I'm right behind you," Chris hollered. "Let's stay to the left side of the slope, so we won't get in anyone's way."

"And vice versa," Gadget added.

"Me next," J.R. said, and took off.

Gadget turned to Stretch. "Wait until I get into position before you start."

"Watch out, A. J. Kitt," Stretch called through cupped gloves. He measured the shady gullies and plotted his attack. Pushing off his edges, and planting his

67

right pole, Stretch sped toward Gadget. With his skis in three-quarter time he powered down to cut and curve around J.R., letting his upper body lead him into the turn around Chris, and then straightening quickly to finish around Jack.

"Wahoo," Jack yelled as Gadget began his run. He didn't push as hard as Stretch, but his technical skill and relaxed approach made him look like a wave rolling onto the shore.

J.R. didn't have as much success. He was nervous and it showed. Instead of leaning forward and bouncing with the slope, he fought it. His legs were straight, and he didn't use his poles to his advantage.

"Watch where you're going?" Jack shouted as J.R. bumped him.

"I'm trying," J.R. called back.

"Sing, J.R., sing," Chris said. "And remember your lesson."

"On top of ol' Smokey," J.R. sang out. With that positive advice, J.R. miraculously improved and was able to use his stem christies around Stretch and Gadget.

"Okay, K-2's, show us your stuff," Jack said to Chris.

Chris was psyched. He stood balanced with his weight on the inside edge of his outside ski drawing a long arc out of his last turn. Then getting his skis out from under his body he pressed his weight to the inside edge of his outside ski. With each turn he flexed his knees and ankles, building up speed and enjoying his newfound energy.

"That was great," J.R. said after Chris finished his turn.

"A nine point eight from the Russian judge," Stretch called, getting ready to start the whole process again.

Gadget held up his hand. "My watch has a stop-watch in it. Let me time you on this one."

The guys had a great time with each run. Stretch won the speed run, with Chris a close second. J.R. had the funniest run, but no one was sure if he was clowning around, or it just happened that way. They stayed in control and out of the way of the rest of the skiers. Before they knew it they were at the bottom of Allan Phipps and Chris hadn't even flinched through the icy spot where he'd fallen the Saturday before.

Gadget's run of choice was Cramner. Stretch chose White Rabbit, while Jack opted for Jabberwocky, and J.R. had his best run on March Hare, which took the gang over to the base of the Olympia lift, the longest lift at the Winter Park resort. Now it was Chris's turn again. He was dying to try Cheshire cat, a blue-black advanced intermediate slope that might be a tough challenge for everyone, especially J.R. "What do you think, guys?" Chris asked hesitantly.

"If you're worried about me, don't," J.R. stated firmly. "I think it's about time that I met the challenge."

"All right," Stretch shouted, having a hard time containing all his energy.

"You don't have to take it, you know, J.R." Jack was actually being kind to his brother.

Gadget took out the trail map and looked at the various slopes. "You could take Jabberwocky or White Rabbit again if you'd like."

"No way," J.R. insisted. "I want to go, really."

"Then let's do it," Chris cheered. The gang swung their poles up in the air and tapped them in the center of the circle where they were standing. "All for one and one for all."

Chapter 8

THE ACCIDENT

"Go, go, go." Chris couldn't contain his excitement. The snow conditions were perfect, the sun was shining and everyone was up about attacking Cheshire cat. The top half of the slope was easy for everyone, but when they met at the ridge and examined the toughest part of the slope, they all became instantly silent.

"Just keep a good rhythm, and ski like you have been all morning," Chris reminded J.R. "You're doing great, and remember you can always stop and rest."

"Right," J.R. said with a forced smile.

"Then let's do it," Chris said with confidence, but before he could start the run, a skier only yards in front of him tumbled hard and slid into a large tree at the edge of the hill.

"That looks bad," Stretch cried.

"I wonder if he needs any help?" Jack asked.

The group forgot about the run and skied to the boy, who lay still in a heap of snow at the base of the tree.

"Are you all right?" Gadget said to the victim.

"I don't think so," the young boy said, barely holding back his tears.

"Where does it hurt?" Stretch continued.

"My ankle," the kid moaned.

"Okay, relax and we'll get you some help." Jack looked around for someone on the ski patrol.

Chris knelt down and picked up the boy's skis, which had come off in the fall. He stabbed one in the snow at an angle, and then jabbed the other in so they crossed. It was a warning to other skiers on the slope.

"That ankle doesn't look too good," Gadget whispered to Stretch. "It could be broken. I think he'll need a toboggan, and some first aid from the ski patrol."

"Right," Stretch agreed.

"Are you skiing with anyone?" Jack asked.

"No, my folks are taking a break down at Snoasis."

"My name's Chris. What's yours?"

"Rick Kincaid," the boy said meekly.

"Okay, Rick, we'll get you some help."

"Thanks," Rick said.

"I'll go for the ski patrol," Stretch volunteered.

"Take Jack with you—you should never ski alone," Chris said, out of the hearing range of Rick.

"You got it," Jack said, agreeing. "We'll meet you on the front porch of Snoasis later. It's probably a good idea to stop for lunch anyway. We'll order for all of you." The two boys skied off.

"Maybe I should try to page the Kincaids at Snoasis and let them know what's happened," Gadget offered.

"Good idea," Chris agreed. "Catch up to the others. J.R. and I will stay here."

"Try to keep him warm and relaxed," Gadget added before calling to Stretch and Jack to wait for him.

"I don't know what happened," Rick said, still dazed. "I started going too fast and I couldn't get control. Before I knew it that tree was coming at me fast."

Chris and J.R. exchanged glances. They'd heard it a thousand times before. Ski within your limits and never lose control. "Help is on the way," Chris said reassuringly.

What seemed like an eternity later, a team of ski patrol members arrived. They pulled a red toboggan and stopped next to the boys. First, one of them asked Rick a series of questions, while another prepared the toboggan for him to ride in. Gently they immobilized his left leg, and then lifted him into the sled. They wrapped blankets around him, laced a canvas cover over the top, and laid his equipment at his side. Only Rick's face was visible. "We'll get him down now," the guy on the ski patrol said, thanking Chris and J.R. After looking up the hill for oncoming skiers, one of the men cautiously took hold of the long double-handled bars in front of the toboggan, while the other took up the rear. They traversed the slope in a modified snow plow and disappeared from view in a matter of minutes.

"Pretty scary stuff," Chris muttered.

"I hope that never happens to me," J.R. whispered back.

"It won't—I'll see to that. Let's go find the others— they'll want to know what's up."

J.R. stood nervously staring down the hill.

"It's okay, J.R., we'll take it real slow. We'll play follow the leader. Do what I do, and we'll be down in no time." Chris decided to take the slope in wide easy turns. He hummed loud enough for J.R. to hear and before long they merged with the other skiers coming off Jabberwocky.

"What do we do now?" J.R. asked, relieved.

"We have to go up on another lift, and then take Butch's Breezeway down to Snoasis." They were quiet on the lift and then continued playing follow the leader down to Snoasis, a warming lodge and cafeteria located on the mountain, halfway between the top of the runs and the base lodge. Chris released his bindings and stepped out of his skis.

"I keep thinking about Rick," J.R. said.

"Me, too. Here, give me one of your skis." Chris reached for one of J.R.'s Blizzards.

"What for?"

"It's a safety precaution. See, if I take one of your skis and poles and put it with mine, and place it on the rack over there, and if you do the same over by the lodge, they'll be safe—no one will steal mismatched skis."

"Pretty clever," J.R. said.

Chris scanned the crowded room and spotted Stretch sitting at a table near the front rail. He released his boots and plodded up the wooden steps. "You guys did a great job, the ski patrol got there really fast."

"I met Rick's folks, and they went down to meet

74

him at the first aid facilities. How's he doing?'' Gadget asked.

"Don't know,'' Chris said.

"I guess we did our good deed for the day, though,'' Jack said.

"I hope I don't ever have to see one of those toboggans again,'' J.R. cried. "It gave me the willies.''

"Let's quit talking about it and have some lunch,'' Stretch said, digging into his fries, "I'm starved.''

"Right,'' Jack added. "We got you all chili and burgers.''

"Thanks,'' Chris said, taking off his hat and gloves.

J.R. did the same and pointed up the hill. "What's that?''

"It's a snow board demonstration, and a couple of the guys are doing aerials on those hills,'' Chris said.

Jack squinted. "Wow, that looks fantastic.''

"I'd like to try it some time,'' Stretch said.

Gadget shook his head. "Not me, I want to keep my feet on the ground.''

"Look that guy just did a double twist in a layout position,'' Chris said.

"You missed the spread eagle and the flips,'' Jack added. "They were awesome.''

"Do you think I could rent one of those snow boards?'' Stretch asked, absorbed by the exhibition.

Before long the High-Fives forgot about Rick and joined the others in the lodge applauding the aerial artists and the snow boarders. They skied more after lunch and ended the day with a series of runs that eventually took them back to the resort.

Chris carefully examined his K-2's and loaded them onto the bus. Except for Rick's accident, it had been an excellent day of skiing. The best part of all was that they hadn't seen the Raiders all day. Chris rested quietly in the comfortable seat on the bus and dreamed about winning an Olympic gold medal in downhill skiing.

Chapter 9

STRANDED

"Do you think they'll cancel on account of the weather," Stretch asked when the High-Fives met the following Saturday outside at the Y.

"They said if the pass is open we can go, but no one's heard a weather report." Gadget walked back to Mrs. Tye to see if she knew anything new.

"It doesn't look good. A lot of kids didn't even show up today," Jack mumbled.

Stretch leaned against the orange brick wall. "Too bad the Raiders weren't some of them."

"They'd go skiing in an avalanche," Chris said.

"One bus has already been cancelled," J.R. added.

"We've got to go," Chris cried. "My dad's letting me rent the lucky skis for another weekend."

J.R. shivered with cold. "I just wish they'd decide so we could get on the bus."

"Load up," Gadget said, returning. "If we leave now we might make it. Mrs. Tye and the bus drivers are willing to try for it."

"Yahoo," Stretch said. The gang rushed to their seats in the back and kept their fingers crossed.

The trip was slow because of the snow, but traffic was light. Most people were staying inside. After three hours of driving through light flurries and a full-blown storm, the Downhillers Club reached the top of the pass that led down to the Winter Park and Mary Jane ski areas.

"Hey, look out the window," Chris called as they started their descent into Winter Park.

"What?" Jack asked, groggy from the long drive. "I don't see anything."

"Precisely," Gadget added.

J.R. blinked his eyes. "Hey, it's not snowing here."

"Creepy," Stretch said, bewildered. "Can it do that?"

"Weather is a very unpredictable element," Gadget said.

"Yeah! We've got a great day of skiing ahead of us." Chris slipped off a shoe and reached into his pack for his ski socks.

"I'll bet the lift lines will be short," Jack cheered.

"Mind if I ski with you guys today?" Alex asked, coming down the aisle and sitting on the armrest of the seat in front of J.R.

"Did your girlfriends chicken out because of the weather?" Jack asked, stretching his legs and resting them on the armrest.

Alex nodded. "In a word, yes."

"It's okay by me," Chris added.

"As long as you can keep up," Jack said.

Alex grinned. "I don't think that'll be a problem."

When the bus pulled into the parking lot, it was only half full. The gang worked like clockwork and were the first skiers on the lift.

All morning Chris continued to ski with confidence, and even began to wedel, a highly precise technique of small turns. He felt as if he could conquer the world, or at least the slopes at Winter Park. After lunch it started snowing, but the gang wasn't ready to stop. They played the human slalom course, and Alex caught on quick. Their race times got faster and faster.

"Let's ski through the trees," Alex suggested when the gang stopped at a cutoff. "It'll be warmer and get us out of the wind and blowing snow."

"What do you mean ski through the trees," J.R. said, gulping.

"Go off course?" Gadget asked.

"Well, it's not like going in an out-of-bounds area," Alex continued. "My ski instructor used to take us in the trees to make us keep our skis closer together. You have to, or you run into a trunk or get stuck."

"I'm willing to try," Gadget said.

"Lead off," Jack said.

Chris was amazed at how hard he had to work to keep on course. The trees formed natural gullies and hills, and he really enjoyed the challenge.

"Whoa," J.R. cried, slipping into a deep drift. "I'm stuck."

Jack went back for his brother. "How in the world did you get your feet behind your head."

"Who knows." J.R. laughed. Without thinking he released his bindings and tried to stand up. Instantly he was hip deep in powder, and really trapped. "Help."

"What did you do now?" Jack groaned.

J.R. struggled with each move. "I thought the only way I'd be able to get up was to take my skis off."

"You thought wrong, huh?" Stretch laughed as he leaned against a tree to watch the struggle.

"Well, are you all going to stand there and laugh, or is someone going to give me a hand?"

They all exchanged glances. "I think we're going to stand here and laugh," Chris said, not moving from his spot.

"This is really deep." J.R. was still struggling.

"I hear you, man," Stretch chuckled. "You figured that when you stand on your skis the snow is solid like the earth."

"It's not, is it, J.R.?" Alex added.

"No, this stuff is like quicksand."

"That's why skis were invented," Gadget began.

"Oh, boy, here comes the lecture," Jack said.

"It's not a lecture," Gadget continued. "But historically, the Nordic countries used skiing for military purposes. Since much of their countries are covered with snow for a large part of the year, they had to find tactical ways of getting around. Hence, cross-country and downhill skiing were invented. Later it became a popular recreational sport."

"Just watching you makes me sweat, J.R." Stretch wiped his forehead and readjusted his headband over his short afro.

"Come on, someone help," J.R. shouted.

"Here," Alex said, extending her gloved hand.

"And grab my pole." Chris pointed the basket end at J.R.

Gadget helped him put on the first ski, and J.R. stepped into the second on his own. "I'm pooped," J.R. said. "Mind if we take a break after this run—or should I say adventure."

"Actually, I'm a little cold, and hot chocolate sounds great." Gadget led the way, pushing into a clearing and onto a run called Little Pierre. "Besides, we have this black advanced slope coming up, and they always wear me out."

"Not me," Chris cheered. "Let's take some air."

"Air," Gadget quizzed. "What is this? I don't like the sound of it."

"Come on, professor," Stretch said, patting Gadget's shoulder. "Live a little."

Jack raised his eyebrows. "Or die early."

"I was afraid of that," Gadget said, forcing a smile.

"It's easy," Chris cried. "When you see a bump, bend your knees even harder than usual, lean forward, and plant your poles in front of you on top of the mound. Then dig in and push off. Watch and learn." Chris went through the exact motions he'd described and soared about three feet into the air. He did a little spread eagle, making an X with his arms and legs, and then landed with a thud on the other side of the mound.

"Way to go," Stretch cheered. "Me next." He attempted a scissor kick jump, but landed on only one foot, and tumbled into the snow. "What a rush," he called, bouncing back onto his feet. "Let's do some more."

Alex was next and she did a very graceful half-turn, landing like a ballerina. The guys applauded.

"Not bad," Jack said. He planted his poles too early, mistiming his leap, and only went about three inches in the air.

"The Russian judge gave you only one point," J.R. teased.

"Let's see what you can do, hot shot," Jack fired back over the laughter.

J.R. nodded and attacked the bump like a pro. He mimicked Chris's movements and completed a spread eagle of his own.

"Beginner's luck," Jack grumbled. "Look at him strut. You'd think he'd just won a gold medal."

"He could, you know," Chris said.

"What?" Stretch asked.

"Win a gold medal. Well, not doing jumps maybe, but at the Nastar races."

"Nastar races?" Gadget questioned.

"Yeah, Winter Park has races here next weekend. It's a slalom course and they award medals."

"Really?" Stretch was intrigued. "Sign me up."

"Not me," Gadget stated.

"Or me," J.R. added. "I'm just learning this stuff. I'm not ready to race."

"You'd be missing out on all the fun," Chris said, urging the gang to sign up.

"I'll think about it. But right now, I want hot chocolate. Last one down the slope buys." Jack pushed off and the others followed. Gadget and J.R. tied for dead last.

It had begun to snow hard and the warming house at the bottom was packed.

"I wonder what's going on. Why's everyone here?" Chris asked, taking J.R.'s left ski and pole. They taught their trick to the others and everyone headed toward the crowd at the information booth.

"We're snowed in." Gadget shouted.

"What?" Alex said, stunned.

Gadget continued. "The pass is blocked, and we have to spend the night here—at least until they get the roads cleared."

"That's great," Stretch cheered.

"Where are we supposed to sleep?" Alex asked.

Stretch did a little dance. "Who's going to sleep. Let's ski all night."

"I have enough trouble not banging into the trees in the daytime," J.R. said, releasing his ankle buckles.

"Just kidding," said Stretch.

"Look, there's my mom." Alex pointed. "Let's find out what we're supposed to do."

"I'm glad you kids are here," Mrs. Tye began. "It appears that we'll be staying tonight."

"At the resort, in the lodge?" Chris asked.

"I guess so. The resort has designated the cafeteria, locker rooms, and warming areas as sleeping zones. I've called some of the parents and they're going to phone the other ones to let them know you're all safe."

"Way cool," Stretch said, unable to control his enthusiasm.

"Why don't we sleep on the bus?" J.R. asked.

"It wouldn't be a good idea." Mrs. Tye motioned for the gang to sit down. "We couldn't keep it heated. You'll be fine in here. Besides, there's a fireplace, restrooms, and plenty of food."

"This is the best adventure the High-Fives have had yet," Chris whispered to Stretch.

"I've made a Downhillers Club sign, and the staff has given me some rope to mark off an area," Mrs. Tye continued, "so we can keep track of everyone. Where would you like to call home for the night?"

Chris was the first to answer. "How about the tables next to the fireplace?"

"Good choice," Stretch said approvingly.

"The picnic tables it is," Mrs. Tye said with a smile. "Alex, why don't you and a couple of the boys help me rope off a section. There are a hundred and twenty of us, so we'll have to plan on a pretty large area."

"J.R. and I owe everyone hot chocolate," Gadget said. "Let's beat the end of the day crowd and bring it back here and help."

Mrs. Tye nodded. "That sounds great, and if you see any other Downhillers, pass the word."

"Check," Gadget said, heading toward the cafeteria.

Chris and the others began roping off about twenty tables, piling their stuff on the one nearest to the fireplace.

"It's really coming down out there," J.R. said as they climbed the stairs to the cafeteria. As they passed the entrance lobby a gust of wind filled it and five figures resembling the abominable snowman clomped in. Gadget knew instantly they were Ron Porter and his Raiders.

"Man, it is freezing out there," Ron gasped, icicles clinging to his hat and clothing.

Greg stomped his boots on the metal grating. "We made it in just in time."

Gadget debated whether to tell them the news, but J.R. beat him to it.

"Guess what?" J.R. asked. "We're stranded."

"Stranded," Randy said, shaking the snow from his jacket.

"Snowed in, more precisely," Gadget corrected. "The pass is closed so we're all spending the night here in the lodge."

The Raiders exchanged glances. "Honest?" Ron asked, taking off his gloves. "Cool."

"Mrs. Tye's got a section for us to sleep by the fireplace," J.R. continued.

"Maybe we'll get stuck up here all winter and they'll have to dig us out in the spring," Hank said, pulling off his gloves.

Peter Farrell unzipped his jacket. "Yeah, think of all the school we'd miss."

Gadget wasn't thrilled about missing school, and nudged J.R. to follow him to the cafeteria. The Raiders shuffled toward the fireplace. When Gadget and J.R. returned, the High-Fives had set up shop, piling coats, hats, and other equipment on a large table in front. The Raiders had chosen the table next to theirs.

"Can't say much about our neighbors," Chris whispered to Gadget, "but it's just for one night." He slipped off the cover on his cocoa and let the steam warm his face.

"What do we do for the rest of the night?" Gadget asked.

"Well, I don't know about you, but after I finish this hot chocolate, I'm going back outside," Stretch said.

"To do what?" Jack wondered. "The lifts are closed."

"Follow me and find out." Stretch took the last two gulps of hot chocolate; put on his hat, coat, and gloves; and grabbed a cafeteria tray before starting for the door.

"Wait for me," Chris called, taking a last sip.

Stretch's face was full of mischief. "You'll need a tray."

"Now he's really got my curiosity up," Gadget added.

"Well, I don't want to sit here all alone," Jack said to J.R., and the brothers followed along.

The High-Fives picked up four more brown plastic trays and rushed out into the blowing snow.

Gadget pulled his turtleneck over his mouth to protect his face from the blowing snow. "If anybody sees us they're going to think we're crazy."

Stretch laughed. "We are, aren't we?"

"The slopes look deserted," Jack said.

"Good, then we won't get in anybody's way." Stretch trudged through the snow toward the nearest slope. He ran partway up the hill and faced the others gawking at him with their mouths open. "Bombs away," he yelled before jumping onto his tray and speeding to the bottom like a bullet.

"Let's go," Chris shouted, rushing up the slope, too.

"Who needs a snow board, I've got a tray." He planted his sneakers on the disc and tried his own method of surfing. A few yards later he tumbled head first into the snow. "This is great."

The others followed and for the next hour, until it started to turn dark, the High-Fives bombed, tumbled, surfed, and tobogganed down the hill on their trays. They even tried linking them together to form a train. It wasn't until Gadget noticed a line of lights heading down the hill toward them that they stopped.

"What's that," Gadget asked.

"It's a U.F.O.," J.R. gasped.

"Or a fire," Jack exclaimed.

"How can there be a fire on a ski slope?" Stretch asked.

"They're skiers," Chris said, making out one member of the ski patrol who was leading a group of staff members down the hill in the early evening snowfall.

"This is awesome," Stretch whispered.

"And pretty, too," J.R. added. "It looks like moving lights on a Christmas tree."

The High-Fives stood together and watched the parade of lights dancing down the slope through the blowing snow. The first member had a torch in his hand, and the others had flashlights.

"Night skiing. I wish we could try that," Chris said.

"I hear the conditions can be icy," J.R. said.

Jack shrugged. "Who cares? It would still be fun."

The guys watched until the last ski patrol member slid past them.

"This has been a great day, guys," Chris said softly. "One of the High-Fives' best."

"But now I'm freezing my buns off," Jack said. "Let's eat."

"Jack's right. Let's go in," Gadget said.

They grabbed their trays and followed the last light into the lodge.

Chapter 10

CAMPING IN

"Hey, where's our junk?" Chris asked, stopping at the table where they had set up for the night.

"Junk is right," Ron Porter said, sitting on the table-top sipping some hot cider.

"This is our table, Porter," Jack snapped.

Randy defended Ron. *"Was* your table."

"Yeah, you guys abandoned it," Peter Farrell added.

"What was wrong with the table you had?" Gadget questioned.

"We like this one better," Greg Forbes said smugly.

Hank Thompson put his feet on the tabletop. "Yeah, it's closer to the fire."

"Well, you can't have it." Jack picked up Ron's jacket and tossed it back toward the other table, which had now been taken over by some of the other Downhillers.

"You can't do that," Ron snapped.

"Oh, really. I think I just did." Jack wasn't giving up any ground.

"Look, we have to spend the night together, we might as well try to get along," Gadget said diplomatically.

Ron shook his head. "Who wants to? You guys left and we moved in. Tough luck."

"We didn't move out, Porter. Our stuff was still here." Chris was practically shouting.

"So, butt out," Jack emphasized.

"Make me," Ron stated.

"You're on, Ron," Jack said, rolling up his sleeves.

"Whoa, hold on a minute," Mrs. Tye called from across the room. "We'll have no fighting tonight. What's the problem?"

"Ron and his buddies took our table," J.R. reported.

"You left," Greg said.

"But we left our gear here, and you jerks threw it all on the floor," Chris said, interrupting.

"If anything's missing you're going to pay, Porter." Jack wasn't about to give up anything.

"All right, everybody settle down." Mrs. Tye held up her arms. "Since Chris and the others helped me set up the area, I think they're entitled to keep the table they first claimed. You fellows will just have to find another spot to spend the night."

"But our table is gone now," Peter Farrell whined.

"Well, I'll talk to them if you'd like," Mrs. Tye continued. "But there is lots of room for everyone. Let's not make this bad situation worse."

"The only thing bad about it is the Raiders," Stretch whispered to Chris.

"Tell me something I don't know," Chris whispered back.

"It's settled, Ron, you and your friends will have to find another place for the night." Mrs. Tye turned around and rejoined Alex.

"You're such a wuss," Ron said, collecting his gear. "You have to have a grown-up do your dirty work for you. But we know what you're really made of. Remember the run on Engledive. Even Mrs. Tye couldn't help you win that battle."

"I'll take you on any time you say, Porter," Chris said.

Randy flexed his muscles. "Sure, you talk big."

Chris stood as tall as he could. "I demand a rematch."

"Any time, Morton, any time." Ron snapped his fingers and pushed his way to another table.

Gadget sighed. "Well I'm glad they're gone, now they won't bother us for the rest of the night."

"Don't count on it, Gadge," Chris whispered. "I say we call an emergency secret High-Fives meeting to plan our attack."

"Attack?" J.R. questioned.

Chris's eyes were serious. "Yep, it's all-out war now." The boys gathered around their table, their heads meeting in the center. With their right hands together they all made a group high-five over the center of the table. "Roll call," Chris whispered over the drone of the crowd. "Thumbs-up."

Jack held up his thumb and tapped the palms of the other guys. "Here."

"Index," Chris muttered.

"Present." Gadget pointed his index finger—his symbol in the High-Five hand—because he was like an index file full of all kinds of information.

"Center," Chris continued.

Stretch ran his middle finger quickly across the other palms. He got his name by being the tallest of the group. "Yo."

"Ringo." Chris nodded, saying his name. He was the ring leader and president of the group. "And P.K., alias Pinky."

"Here," J.R. said as the youngest and smallest member. He liked using his initials. He tapped his little finger against the others' palms.

The boys stared at one another and drummed their fingertips on the tabletop, then each High-Five slapped the hand of the guy to his right, grabbed hands, and wriggled his fingers.

"I've called this meeting because I think we have to take some immediate action," Chris said in a low, serious voice.

Jack cleared his throat. "First off, we can't leave this table unguarded at any time."

"Do you think we should sleep in shifts?" J.R. asked.

"I don't think it's that serious, but they could try to pull anything," Chris added. "We have to go and lock our skis and equipment in the bus." The gang nodded.

Stretch looked over his shoulder. "And then I think we should plan the rest of the evening."

"Stretch and J.R., you get the food after we put the equipment away. J.R. and I will stand guard."

"We'll go to the bathroom in pairs and never all at the same time." Stretch was totally involved now.

"Now you're thinking," Chris said with a smile.

"And most important, don't let any of them corner you. They may be out for blood," Jack added.

"Everyone got the plan straight?" Chris said. "Then the meeting's over. We'll get the minutes from Gadget next time, and any other business we need to cover. Meeting adjourned."

The evening went well. The High-Fives enjoyed their burgers and fries. They used their sweaters and jackets as pillows and blankets and gathered by the fire for one last hot chocolate and one of Stretch's famous ghost stories. The Raiders were quiet and left them alone.

Chapter 11

AVALANCHE

The following morning the sun shone brightly through the large windows of the lodge. J.R. hadn't slept much—Stretch's ghost story had been too realistic. The daylight was a welcome sight to him.

"Hey look, guys," J.R. said, pointing out to the deep powder outside the windows.

Stretch rolled over from his spot on top of the table. "Let's hit the slopes."

Jack rubbed his eyes. "Yeah, I've never skied in new powder."

"We should eat something first, right, Chris?" Gadget said, reminding everyone of what happened on the first trip.

"Fine, no problem," Chris said, grabbing his backpack. "I still have my mom's sack lunch from yesterday. It's not a lot, but we'll split it so we won't have to fight the crowds in the cafeteria."

"Let's eat," Jack cried. "We can stop for more food later."

Chris divided up the goodies. "You know what I want to do?"

"What?" Stretch said, taking the potato chips.

Chris cut the sandwich into sections. "I want to take a run we've never taken before."

Jack bit into his slice of bologna sandwich. "Yeah, a long run so we'll have to go all the way to the top."

"There's only one problem," J.R. said.

"Don't spoil it, J.R.," Gadget added.

"I'm not. It's just that I don't have enough money for another tow ticket for the day."

"You don't need one," Chris said, trying to figure out how to divide his Snickers bar into five even pieces.

"Since we're stranded, the Winter Park resort association will give us free tickets for the day." Stretch took a swig from a warm Coke.

"We'd better check with Mrs. Tye and find out for sure." Gadget slipped on his glasses, reached into his coat pocket, and tossed his trail map onto the table. "I'll see if she's awake and ask her. You guys figure out the mystery run."

Chris glanced at the map. "The best one would be Sleeper, but it's over the hill at the Mary Jane resort."

"Don't they have a shuttle to Mary Jane?" Chris asked.

"I think so," J.R. said.

"That's it then. If there's a shuttle, we go to Mary Jane."

"Guess which hand," Gadget said, returning to the gang, his hands behind his back and a big grin on his face.

"The right," Stretch said.

"The left," Chris topped.

Jack pounced forward, toppling Gadget to the bench. "Both." He grasped Gadget's hands and pulled out five lift tickets. "That settles it—we're going skiing."

"Thanks for the wake-up call, Jack," Gadget said, pulling himself together. "Mrs. Tye said that the roads are still blocked, but the plows are heading out now to clear them. We're supposed to check back here at noon, but until then, the slopes are ours. So where am I going to break my leg today?"

"Over at Mary Jane," J.R. said nervously.

"I think I can do it. Are we taking the shuttle? They leave every fifteen minutes from the parking lot."

"Then we're going to be on the next one." Stretch jumped up.

Chris agreed. "Look, everybody's getting up now. The cafeteria will open in a little while, so let's get our gear and get moving." The guys rallied and before most of the other skiers had their boots on, the High-Fives were riding the shuttle to Mary Jane.

"I've never skied on Mary Jane," J.R. said, staring at the trail map.

"It's the same concept as Winter Park, stupid," Jack groaned. "You put your skis on and go down the hill."

"I know that, but most of the slopes there are advanced ones."

"Sidetrack and Sleeper are blue-blacks, and you've skied blue-blacks." Chris tried to sound reassuring.

"We can take it real easy," Gadget said. "If the

96

speed demons want to race, we'll meet them at the bottom."

The day had become overcast with sunshine breaking through the clouds. It was cold, but the sun was warm. Since the Summit chair lift was an express, the High-Fives were at the top in eight minutes.

"I've dreamed about doing this for years," Chris said, tightening his boots. "To be the first ones down in the morning."

"Well, well, well. Look what the wind blew in," Ron Porter said, skiing up next to the High-Fives.

"What run are you guys planning to take?" Ron asked.

"Whichever one you're not," Stretch stated.

Ron crossed his arms over his chest. "Well, how do you like that. Here I am trying to be friendly and you're nasty."

"We're taking Sleeper," J.R. blurted out.

"What'd you have to tell him for," Jack whined.

Ron nodded his head. "Not a bad run, but nothing like Derailer, or better yet, one of the bowls over the ridge."

"Those are in the out-of-bounds area," Gadget stated.

"Out of bounds for rookie skiers maybe but not us pros. Right, guys? Right, Morton?" Ron continued.

Gadget sidestepped to Chris. "We can't ski over there, Chris, it's marked off. It's beyond the boundaries of the resort."

Chris didn't react to either boy's statement.

"Yeah, we're going to take it. New snow, deep,

white powder, just begging to be skied." Greg sniffed the air.

"You're not thinking of going, are you, Chris?" J.R. asked.

"Why shouldn't he?" Ron urged. "He's got fancy equipment now. He should be a top-notch skier. This is the perfect way to prove it."

Gadget was serious. "Chris, there are avalanche warning signs posted all over the place. You can't do this."

Randy shrugged his shoulders. "Hey, we do it all the time."

"If you get caught, they'll take your ticket away," J.R. said.

"So who's going to get caught?" Greg asked.

"Well, you can count me out," Gadget said boldly.

"Me, too," J.R. echoed.

Ron kept urging. "Do something daring for once in your life, Morton. Ditch these beginners and show us what you're made of."

"Who are you calling a beginner?" Jack said defensively.

"You, if you're too scared to take a challenge," Hank said.

"A challenge is one thing, stupidity's another," Stretch said.

"You going to let those guys make your decisions for you?" Ron continued.

Chris looked over at the avalanche signs and the ropes marking off the boundaries. "No, Porter, I'm going to let the rules tell me what to do."

"Thank heavens," Gadget muttered.

"Chicken, chicken, chicken," Ron and the others started clucking like hens in a coop.

"Come on, Chris, let's stick with the game plan." Jack pivoted around and headed for the start of their run.

"You guys go ahead," Chris said to the other High-Fives, "I'll catch up with you later."

"You're not going to go with them, are you?" Stretch asked.

"Just go ahead," Chris shouted impatiently, not moving from his spot.

"Just go," Chris repeated.

"Let's go, guys," Stretch said, leading the High-Fives away.

"We'll wait for you at the top of the run," Gadget added.

Chris waited until the High-Fives were out of earshot. "Let's settle this once and for all, Porter."

"Great, let's go," Ron agreed.

"Not here and not now. The Nastar races next Saturday."

Ron's grin broadened. "Now this could be interesting. You're on—with one condition."

"Name it." Chris's expression stayed unchanged.

"The whole gang competes. The Raiders against the High-Fives. Or don't you think everyone's up to it."

"They can do it."

"Losers carry the winners' equipment back and forth to the bus for the rest of the season."

Chris knew he couldn't flinch. It had been his challenge and he would just have to find a way to convince the others that this was the best way to settle everything. "Deal."

The two leaders shook hands and then Chris watched Ron and the other Raiders slide under the out-of-bounds ropes. Chris stood for a moment, trying to decide whether to follow them. It really would be the ultimate experience. He paused for a moment and then pushed off.

"I still don't see him." Stretch strained to spot Chris coming down the slope. The group had stopped at the Mary Jane resort base lodge.

"And it's been over half an hour," Gadget added.

Jack shook his head. "I can't believe Porter convinced him to go in the out-of-bounds area."

"We don't know for sure that he did," J.R. said.

"Yeah, well, what explanation do you have?" Jack continued. "We could've skied three runs by now. He's got to be with Ron."

"Maybe he got lost," Gadget suggested.

"Nice try," Jack said with a smirk.

"Hey, look, there's Alex. Maybe she's seen him." Gadget raised his pole into the air and caught Alex's attention. She skated over to the group.

"Hi, guys. Great day for skiing. What's up?"

"Have you seen Chris?" Stretch asked.

"No, why? Isn't he skiing with you."

"Not exactly," Stretch said under his breath.

"We think he may have gone skiing with the Raiders in an out-of-bounds area," J.R. said.

"Yeah, where they posted avalanche warnings," Jack added.

"That doesn't sound like Chris." Alex paused for a moment. "Except Porter has a way of getting to Morton." She shook her head. "So what do you want to do?"

Gadget continued. "We're trying to decide whether to tell the ski patrol, or try to find him on our own."

"We can find him," Jack suggested. "We should at least give it a shot. Take out your map, Gadget."

Gadget unzipped his side pocket and took out the trail map that showed the one hundred and six designated trails on the one thousand, one hundred and five acre area that made up the Winter Park and Mary Jane resorts. "Maybe we should check at the first aid station again, just in case he's had an accident."

"I'll go, and you guys make a plan." Alex dug her poles deep in the snow and headed to the small building where a red flag with a white cross on it was flapping in the breeze.

"If there are no objections," Gadget stated seriously, "I think we should stay in pairs. J.R. and I will take our original Sleeper run, and Stretch, Alex, and Jack can attempt to find him on Derailer or Rail Bender."

Stretch buckled his boots. "Okay, let's just get going."

J.R. slipped on his pole straps. "Yeah, remember we're supposed to meet at the Winter Park base lodge at noon."

"Hey, maybe if Chris got lost he went there," Stretch said.

Jack nodded. "Could be."

"Sounds logical," Gadget added. "We'll check it out."

Alex skied back to the gang, "Bad news, guys."

"Chris is hurt," J.R. exclaimed. "I knew it."

"No, no, hold on, it's not that. I wish it were that easy."

"This must be bad if you wish Chris had been hurt," Gadget said quietly.

"Come on, Alex, tell us what's wrong," J.R. pleaded.

Alex sighed deeply. "There's been an avalanche on the back side of Mary Jane."

Stretch gasped. "Oh, man, that's where they were going."

"The ski patrol didn't have reports of any injuries, but there were some ski tracks, so they're looking."

"How many tracks?" Jack demanded.

"I don't know, I didn't stick around to find out."

Gadget's voice was quiet. "Do you think we should tell the patrol about Chris and the Raiders?"

"Probably," Jack said with a sigh. "But I'd like to check the slopes and the tracks before we get anybody into trouble."

"Then let's move it," Stretch said. "We'll stick with Gadget's plan and pray that Chris shows up."

In record time the gang mobilized and were on the same chair lift to the top. "What's it like to be caught in an avalanche?" J.R. asked Gadget as they rode back up to the top.

"Well, from what I've read, it feels like a strong wave of snow. If you get caught in one you should try to swim or body surf your way to the top. If you do get covered, don't panic, and the first thing you should do is spit or drool.''

"Why?"

"It could save your life. If, in fact, the snow has tossed you around like a wave, and covered you, you may not know which way is up. If you drool and it heads toward your chin, you know to start digging out over your head. But you may have landed upside down, in which case your spit would head for your forehead. You'll need to start digging the opposite way your saliva runs.''

"This whole thing is spookier than Stretch's story.''

"That's because it's real. Some resorts, especially in Europe, have skiers wear beepers if they're skiing in an area susceptible to avalanches.''

"I wish Chris had one.'' The boys were quiet for the rest of the ride. They met the others at the crest and stared silently into the out-of-bounds area.

"There are more than five tracks into the zone,'' Alex said.

Stretch tried to see down the hill. "I can't tell if Chris or the Raiders actually went in.''

"The tracks could belong to the ski patrol,'' Alex added.

"It's all that new wet snow,'' Gadget agreed. "An avalanche was inevitable.''

"Let's get going,'' Jack said. "This gives me the creeps. Besides, we're not doing Chris any good standing here. If he is caught in that stuff, he needs help now. If he's not, we still have to report him and the

Raiders missing to the ski patrol, and then head down to the Winter Park resort and tell Mrs. Tye."

Even more determined, the gang pushed off toward their appointed runs. Suddenly a shrill but familiar-sounding whistle jolted everyone's attention. "Hey, guys, wait up," Chris panted. "I've been looking all over for you."

"Where have you been?" Jack demanded.

"We were waiting for you at the bottom in front of the Mary Jane lodge," J.R. added.

Stretch topped the others in volume. "I thought you weren't going to go with the Raiders."

"There's been an avalanche," Gadget stated.

"What, wait, slow down, one at a time," Chris said. "I got lost."

"Lost?" J.R. asked, and sighed. "So you didn't go out of bounds with the Raiders?"

"No way. I told you I wasn't going to. I'm not stupid."

"What were we supposed to think when you didn't show," Jack snapped. "Where'd you end up?"

"Actually in a great area—very few people are skiing there. It's all blue intermediate runs, perfect for you, J.R. I took a run called Edelweiss, which took me to another lift called Sunnyside."

Gadget had the map open. "Here it is, way over here on the Mary Jane side."

Chris continued. "I thought I saw Jack's ski parka going down a run called Bluebell. By the time I caught up with the kid and her friends, I was lost."

"Her!" Jack cried. "You mistook me for a girl?"

"Sorry." Chris shrugged. "I took a blue-black slope back down to Mary Jane. You guys weren't around, so I came back up here."

"Boy, are we glad to see you." J.R. patted Chris's shoulder. "We were about to report you and the Raiders missing to the ski patrol. We thought you were caught in the avalanche."

"You mean you thought—" Chris started.

"Look, it's almost noon," Gadget interrupted. "We're supposed to meet the Downhillers at Winter Park. I say we get the lead out. If the Raiders aren't there, we'll report them missing to the ski patrol."

Everyone agreed, and the High-Fives and Alex made it down to the Winter Park base in record time.

"Well, it's noon now," Jack said, checking out the clock tower. "There's no sign of them anywhere."

"I'll go tell my mom," Alex said.

"Maybe they're just late," J.R. said.

"Or dead," Jack added.

In minutes Mrs. Tye, two ski patrol members, and the rest of the Downhillers Club were standing outside the patrol office.

"The ski patrol said there were no signs of skiers in any of the avalanche areas," Mrs. Tye explained. "The avalanche was only a small one, but they're going to send up another unit to check out the spot you boys last saw them. It's twelve-thirty now, the roads are clear, and the bus is ready. Let's pack up and be ready to leave as soon as the lost boys show up."

"What lost boys?" Ron asked, skiing to the back of the group.

J.R. stared ahead, still listening to Mrs. Tye. "Stupid ol' Ron Porter and his idiot friends."

"Who are you calling stupid?" Ron shouted.

J.R. spun around. "Ron, you're all right." Mrs. Tye stopped talking and the club members turned to see Ron and the rest of the Raiders standing behind them.

"Of course we're all right. We're just a little late, that's all. No big deal."

"We thought you were caught in an avalanche in the out-of-bounds area," Chris added.

"You told the ski patrol that we skied in an out-of-bounds area?" Ron grumbled.

"All right, all right, let's settle down," Mrs. Tye said, walking back to the boys. "Everybody get on the bus, except for Ron and his friends. The ski patrol and I would like to talk to you for a few minutes in the office."

Ron slipped off his skis and crossed to Chris, while the rest of the club started to shuffle toward the parking lot. "If we get into trouble, tattletale, you'd better pray your skis have wings, because you're going to need them to beat us in the Nastar races next week."

Chapter 12

TO RACE OR
NOT TO RACE

"So, Stretch, are you getting excited about the Nastar races this weekend?" Chris asked his friend as the boys walked down the hall of Dugan Junior High between classes.

"I never said I was going to race," Stretch answered. "Besides, I rented a ski board from your dad for this weekend. I can't wait to try it out."

"But the race is the best. You don't want to miss it."

"Maybe another weekend." Stretch patted Chris on the back.

"But this weekend is when we said we were going to race." Chris couldn't tell him that he'd already made a bet with Ron.

"What race?" Jack said, joining them at Stretch's locker.

"The Nastar races." Chris used his hands and painted a visual picture. "You want to race, don't you, Jack? The rush of competition, the thrill of the challenge, the smell of gold."

"Gold?" Jack asked.

"Yeah," Chris continued. "They give out medals, just like at the Olympics. You could be wearing a gold medal next week."

"Sure, great. I'm in," Jack said, getting his history book.

"All right," Chris cheered. "So how about you, Stretch? Come on, you don't want to miss the fun."

"Sorry, Chris, another weekend. I'm snow-boarding."

"But, Stretch—" Chris started to say. The bell rang and the boys bustled to their history class.

Chris couldn't concentrate. He had to figure out a way to convince Stretch to postpone his snow-boarding without telling him about the bet. Ron wouldn't give up, so Chris had to deliver.

The Raiders had gotten a stiff reprimand from the ski patrol, but their passes weren't taken away. Ron explained to the patrol that they'd gone under the rope, but after looking at the hill, they'd turned back and skied Phantom Bridge instead. Their tracks substantiated the story, so they were let off easy and didn't lose their skiing privileges. Instead, they would have to go to a lecture on ski safety at Winter Park the afternoon of the club's final outing.

Chris decided to work on Gadget and J.R. If he could convince them, Stretch would come around. Since he wouldn't see J.R. until after school, Gadget was his best shot.

"Gadget, ol' buddy," Chris said, stepping up next to his friend after history. "Is there anything I can help you with?"

"I beg your pardon?" Gadget asked.

"Here we go again," Stretch said, knowing what was up. "Don't let him talk you into anything."

"You stay out of this, Stretch," Chris said, pulling on Gadget's arm. "Just because you're going to miss the greatest rush the High-Fives have ever had, that doesn't mean Gadget has to."

"What are you talking about?" Gadget asked.

"The Nastar races at Winter Park this weekend," Chris said.

"Races? Oh, I don't think so, Chris. I'm not the racing type."

"What do you mean you're not the racing type? I've seen you compete before. Remember when you wanted to be a quarterback? You proved you were a major competitor. Come on," Chris begged. "What do you say?"

"Look, Chris, I know you really want to do this, and I think you should. It's just not for me. Besides, I'm going to do some cross-country skiing next to Winter Park this weekend. I'm selling my tow ticket to a kid in our P.E. class. Mrs. Tye said there was enough room on the bus for him to ride up. I'm really looking forward to a calm, quiet, invigorating day cross-country skiing."

"What?" Chris couldn't hide his disappointment. "Come on, Gadge, you can cross-country in Conrad. Don't sell your ticket."

"It's just one day. I'll ski with you the next weekend."

"Please, Gadget, cross-country the weekend after?"

"Hey, quit pressuring the guy," Stretch pleaded. "If racing is that important to you, you can wait for another Saturday."

"I can't," Chris mumbled.

"Why not?" Stretch asked.

Chris sighed. "I have my heart set on this weekend."

"Well un-set it and relax," Stretch said.

At the end of the day Chris stood in the middle of the hall, thinking. He had to get them all to race on the weekend, he just had to. Slowly a smile came across his face. "J.R.," he whispered to himself. "If I can convince J.R., Gadget might change his mind and then Stretch will come over, and we'll be set." He clapped his hands together, and with new enthusiasm, headed for the exit, and a pep talk with J.R. He quickened his pace, knowing he'd have to work fast to get him to agree before the others showed up for their usual after-school gathering at Mike's Diner.

"Hey, J.R., what's happening?" Chris said, spying his friend about to enter Mike's.

"Hi, Chris," J.R. said. "Where's everybody else?"

"They're coming. I wanted to talk to you for a minute."

"Sure, what's up?"

"I wanted to tell you how good you're doing on the slopes."

"Thanks, I had a good teacher." The boys pushed

open the big green door and headed for their booth in the back.

"No, you deserve a lot of credit. And now I think you're ready for a new challenge."

"Really, what?"

"The Nastar races this weekend."

"Race, what kind of race?"

Chris's enthusiasm rose. "It's a slalom course consisting of twelve to fifteen gates. Two race officials run the course first and set a time. Since we're in the youngest age group, we get a few seconds handicap to match that time. Depending on how fast you are, and if you don't miss any gates or fall down, you can win medals just like in the Olympics. They award gold, silver, and bronze. It's got to be the greatest. You can win a gold medal."

"Do you think I'm ready?"

"Of course you are."

"I think maybe I'll watch. Maybe I can do it another time."

"Another time? J.R., there's nothing to be afraid of. You owe it to yourself to give it a try."

"Maybe, but I think I'll just watch, anyway."

Chris sat back, frustrated. "I can't believe you're scared."

"I'm not scared, I'm just not interested. Not yet at least."

Stretch had come in and was now unzipping his coat and scooting into the booth. "Still talking up the races, huh, Chris?"

"Yeah, and why not?" Chris sounded defensive. "I

think they'll be a blast. I can't believe I have to try to talk you into it."

"I agree," Jack said, sliding in next to Chris. "It's an opportunity to do something different and fun."

"Exactly," Chris agreed. "Listen to Jack."

Gadget stared down at the tabletop. "Maybe the last weekend. They're having them then, too."

"Right," Stretch acknowledged.

Chris shook his head. "Don't put off until tomorrow what you can do today."

"You sound like my mother," Stretch groaned.

"Well, maybe you should listen to her," Chris fired back.

"Hi, guys, ready for next weekend?" Alex stepped up to the table. "The weather is supposed to be great— new snow."

"Perfect racing conditions," Chris said.

"Cool it, Chris. We'll do your silly race, just not this weekend," Stretch said.

"Why not?" Chris asked as he looked at their blank faces. "I give up," Chris said as he slumped deeper into his seat.

"Good, now we can at least eat in peace," Gadget said, playing with the salt shaker.

"So what'll you guys have?" Alex asked even though she knew the answer.

"The usual," everyone except Chris bellowed.

The rest of the week Chris tried but failed to win J.R., Gadget, and Stretch over. He was quiet on the bus trip up, and wondered what he was going to tell Ron and the Raiders when they met at the starting gate.

"What's with Chris," Alex asked. She was unloading her gear from the luggage compartment.

"He's still bummed out about this race thing," J.R. replied.

Gadget hoisted his cross-country skis. "I can't figure out why he's so persistent."

Alex agreed. "He's crazed about the whole thing."

"I tried to avoid him all week," Stretch said.

"There's got to be something else going on," Jack said.

Stretch nodded. "Yeah, and I think we should find out what it is."

"But how?" Alex asked.

"Well, if he won't tell us, let's investigate," Gadget said.

Chris silently gathered his nerve and equipment and headed for the chair lift alone. He'd decided to tell Ron the truth. The High-Fives weren't up for racing. He stalled by taking a few runs to figure out what to say. He could hear the razzing that Porter would give him from then until the spring thaw, not to mention carrying the Raiders' equipment. Finally, when he knew he couldn't wait any longer, he found Porter waiting for him at the start of the course.

"It's about time you showed up," Ron said.

"The lift lines were long at the bottom," Chris lied.

"Well, where's the rest of your puny pack?"

Chris stared at the snow and cleared his throat. "I need to talk to you about that."

"Chicken, right?" Porter said, laughing.

"They're not chicken, they just have things to do first."

"Like blow their noses and figure out how to put on their skis."

"Very funny," Chris said.

"We need to set the ground rules, so where are they?"

"Right here," Stretch said, schussing up and spraying Ron with a shower of snow.

"Yeah, keep your shorts on," Jack said, coming up next.

"We don't see the rest of your buddies," J.R. stated as he followed Jack. "Aren't they going to race today?"

"Yeah, who's chicken around here?" Gadget asked as he arrived on the scene. "We've been primed for this competition all week."

Stretch rested his arms on his poles. "Probably too scared to show up."

Chris couldn't say a word. He was so proud of the High-Fives, the best group of friends any guy ever had.

Chapter 13

THE RACE

"I don't know what to say," Chris said after Ron skied away to gather the rest of the Raiders.

"Why didn't you tell us you made a bet with Porter?" Stretch asked.

"Yeah, you know we wouldn't back down from a challenge," Jack added.

"Gadget, what about your cross-country ski day? Or your snow-boarding, Stretch?" Chris asked. "I don't want to spoil your special days just because I shot my big mouth off."

"We talked it over," Gadget said with a smile. "This is more important."

"What about you, J.R.?" Chris questioned.

"I may not be able to help you out very much, but I'll do my best. I can't let my coach or the High-Fives down."

"I don't know how to thank you," Chris said, embarrassed. "How did you find out?"

J.R. pointed. "Alex is the one you need to thank."

"Alex?" Chris stared at the tall girl standing in back of the gang.

Alex explained. "I overheard Peter and Randy talking about the race and the bet. The losing team has to carry the other team's equipment, right? I told the others and then they decided to race."

Chris was very grateful to Alex. "I hope you decided to race because you wanted to, not just because of the equipment thing."

"Nah, because of the challenge," Stretch said.

Chris smiled. "Thanks, I owe you."

Stretch clapped his gloved hands together. "Okay, super skier, tell us what we need to do."

"Let's figure out a game plan," Jack cried.

Chris sighed. "Well, first off, we need to register with the Nastar officials." He pointed to the starting gate and explained the course. "This is a regular slalom course, rather than a super Nastar course. There are twelve gates and two courses, you race in pairs. See, one run has blue flags and the other has red. They're the same, it just gives you someone to race against. We'll take each course once."

"I'm psyched," Stretch said.

"How do you know when to start?" J.R. asked.

Chris continued. "One of the officials will count you down. You know—five, four, three, two, one, go. Actually your race time doesn't start until you trip the timer wand with your skis. The official time ticks off on the digital clock at the finish line."

"Does everybody know your race time?" Gadget asked.

"Yes, but don't let that shake you," Chris replied. "You always have the second run to redeem yourself."

"What if you fall down or miss a gate?" Alex inquired.

"You're disqualified for any run where you miss a gate," Chris answered. "You might even get penalty time added on, but don't worry about it. The most important thing is to have fun."

"That's a little tough to do with the Raiders breathing down our necks," Jack grumbled.

"Try to think of it as a race against the clock and yourself," Chris suggested.

Stretch slapped his gloves together. "Hey, it's just like our human slalom course, but with real gates. Not fence gates, they're just poles with flags on them stuck in the snow."

"Right, and we've all done that," Chris added.

Alex pointed to the course. "What's that snow plow doing?"

Chris stomped his skis in the snow. "It's getting the snow prepared. Which reminds me, I've already waxed my skis for wet-packed snow. If anybody wants to borrow some wax, it's in my pack."

"I'll use some if you don't mind," Jack said.

"Be my guest," Chris added. "I guess we'd better sign up. The earlier we run the course, the better times we'll get."

"How come?" Alex asked.

"We won't have to race in another person's ruts. It'll

probably get icier, too. I don't know about you guys, but I'm not so hot on ice." Chris slipped on his pole straps.

"Hey, the snow plows must be finished, they're resetting the poles," Jack said, adjusting his goggles.

"We'd better hustle. The officials will be running the course in a minute to set the par time," Chris said.

The High-Fives and Alex skied to the bottom of the course and registered at the timing house, a small building up the slope from Snoasis.

"I'm going for two golds," Jack bragged.

"I just hope to finish," J.R. mumbled.

The gang each paid a five-dollar entrance fee and tied on an orange plastic vest that had a number printed on it.

"Do you think number twenty-seven is a lucky number?" Stretch asked, slipping on his vest.

"I hope ten is," Alex added.

"And twenty-five," Gadget topped.

"How come I'm only number nine?" J.R. asked.

"Because you're short," Stretch teased.

"Very funny," J.R. answered with a sneer.

"Well, I have lucky number seven, so I know I'm going to do well," Chris said, proudly tying the last knot of his vest.

"You're going to need more than a lucky number to save you, Morton," Ron said, skiing with his group toward the High-Fives.

Randy did a kick turn on his skis. "I hope J.R.'s strong enough to carry my stuff."

"I'm not worried," J.R. said boldly. "Especially because I'm not going to be carrying it."

"Hey, she doesn't count," Peter said, pointing to Alex.

"Why not?" Chris asked. "Afraid she might beat you?"

"No, because she's a girl. Besides it's the five of us against the five of you." Greg Forbes added.

"Don't sweat it, Forbes," Alex said. "I'm not interested in your stupid bet. I'm racing purely for the fun of it."

"Is there such a thing?" Jack whispered to Gadget.

Hank leaned on his poles. "Too bad your pals won't be able to do the same."

"I see you have your prize K-2's on again," Ron said, a little enviously.

"Scared, huh?" Chris's voice rang out with confidence.

"In your dreams." Ron pretended to take a gate. "I'll do my talking on the course. See you at the top." He glided away.

The two groups separated to ride up the chair lift, with Chris lagging behind. He had to double-check his bindings.

"Any last-minute tips, coach?" J.R. asked, joining him. "My knees are shaking so hard, I won't make it out of the gate."

Chris stomped his skis in the snow. "You'll do fine, J.R. Give yourself some credit. To be honest, I don't care if we win or not. Just the fact that you guys showed up is a win for me."

"Me, too," J.R. agreed.

119

"Let's go kick some butt," Jack cheered.

Chris and J.R. rode up the lift in silence, watching the officials take the time run. Chris turned around to see the digital time charted on a sign by the finish line. With their age-range handicap, the guys would have to score less than forty-five seconds for a gold, forty-six to fifty to win a silver, and fifty-one to fifty-five seconds to receive a bronze.

"Guess who's up first?" Stretch whispered to Chris when they arrived at the starting house. "J.R. drew Ron."

"Number nine and number twelve," one of the officials called. Ron and J.R. slid forward. "And numbers twenty-seven and fourteen are on deck." Stretch and Peter followed them.

J.R. stiffly positioned himself in the starting gate.

"Now don't fall," Ron teased. "I know you just got your training skis off."

J.R. didn't say a word, but focused on the red flags in front of him. Suddenly he heard the word *go,* and the race was on. Ron pushed off with full force, pulling ahead immediately. J.R. just leaned forward and slid for the first flag.

With an easy rhythm, Ron met each gate with effortless aggression. Meanwhile, J.R. faltered twice, practically snow plowing around each gate. Ron zoomed over the finish line with a forty-four second time, and the first gold medal for the Raiders. He stopped long enough to cheer and then turned back and yelled at J.R.

"If you turn any wider, Klipp, you'll cross the state line into Wyoming," Ron cheered.

Greg continued the razzing. "Maybe he thinks he's supposed to get a big score like in bowling."

J.R. was humiliated with his minute-and-twelve-second time.

"We may as well give up now," Stretch grumbled.

Chris refused to be defeated. "There's a lot of skiing to do before we give up. Come on, Stretch, get a gold."

Stretch crouched in the starting gate; he was paired with Peter. He bolted out over the wand and attacked the red gates like a pro, leaning gracefully into each marker and edging around the curves in quick rhythmic motions. Stretch stayed low between gates and had a finish time of forty-three seconds. The High-Fives had their first gold.

"Way to go," Jack shouted down the hill.

"All right, Evans!" Alex echoed.

"This is what we needed to get us going again." Chris's excitement grew.

Peter Farrell had finished the run in fifty-eight seconds. Better than J.R., but not good enough to get any medal.

After a few runs by kids the gang didn't know, Jack, on the red course, was pitted against Randy Salazar on the blue.

"Get ready to eat my snow," Jack said to Randy before standing on the starting mound.

"Just stay on your skis, Klipp," Randy said.

Jack was fueled with a combination of anger and pride. He was proud that his brother had overcome his fears, and finished the run, but he felt responsible for making up for the bad time. He raced the red course well. Not as smooth as Stretch, but with enough power to win a silver at forty-nine seconds. Randy skied like his shadow but only took a bronze with fifty-four seconds.

Alex took on a girl and finished with the same time as Stretch to earn a gold. Now it was Gadget's turn on the red against Hank on the blue.

Chris gave him a pep talk as he waited for the countdown. "Technically, you're a great skier. Keep all of those facts in your head and concentrate on controlled speed. Don't be afraid to be aggressive. You did it in football, now do it on the snow."

"I'll give it my best," Gadget said, focusing on the red gates. And race he did, finishing the course with a forty-seven-second run to earn a silver, beating Hank by three seconds. He pulled off his glasses and greeted the High-Fives who were at the finish line. "I was so nervous, I forgot my goggles. I went as fast as I could because I was afraid my glasses would totally fog up before I finished."

"Whatever you did, it worked," J.R. cheered.

"Yeah, hide this guy's goggles," Stretch said.

"Or make sure he puts them on," Alex added. "He may break the course record if he wears them."

Chris stood anxiously waiting at the top of the hill. He wished he were finished and could be at the bottom, congratulating Gadget. He had to put in a good time, not just because J.R. hadn't earned a medal, but because he was the reason the gang was there. They were having fun, but he had forced them to change their plans for the day, and he wanted to make it worth their effort.

If the High-Fives ended up carrying the Raiders' equipment, it would be his fault, not J.R.'s.

While another race was going on, Chris tried to create a psychological edge. He closed his eyes and imagined the gates. Using his hands he skied through the course, bending into each gate and rising gently through each turn. He visualized his edges slicing the snow and speeding toward the finish line. When he opened his eyes, he felt calm and ready to go. Even though he was paired with Greg, he tuned out his comments about the bunny hill or his fall on Engledive hadn't fazed his confidence and composure. Chris stared at the first red gate. He would take them one at a time—he hoped for the gold.

Chris lurched forward, tripping the wand. His muscles tensed and he felt stiff going around the first gate. Relax, he told himself, remembering his visual run, and the tension oozed from his limbs, and he picked up his pace and poise. The sound of Greg's skis cutting the edges rang in his head. Bend and up and bend and shift, he said to himself. He could see the final gate rising ahead of him, so he crouched lower and powered around it. Tucking his poles under his armpits, he bent lower to pick up valuable seconds at the finish. The crowd cheered, and he felt as if he'd done well, but he couldn't see or hear the actual results.

"Nice run." Stretch rushed up to him.

"That'll help our standings a lot," Jack echoed.

"A silver this time. A gold next time," Gadget said.

Chris bent over and grabbed his knees, gasping for air. It had only been forty-six seconds, but he felt spent and exhausted.

"It's harder than it looks," Alex said, patting his back.

Chris bent over farther and released his bindings. Greg had beaten him by a second, enough for a gold. "We've got about an hour before our next run. Let's get something to drink and tally up the times."

Alex waved goodbye. "I'll see you guys later then. I've got a friend coming down the course in a few minutes."

"I think I'll wait out here and watch for a while," J.R. said, carrying his skis.

"Nothing doing," Jack replied, slinging an arm around his brother's shoulder. "You raced just as hard as the rest of us, and you deserve a break. Besides, we have to talk about the blue course. You'll be skiing that one next."

J.R. was happy to have his brother's support. "I didn't think you'd want me to ski again."

"Hey, don't talk like that," Gadget said. "Remember the High-Five motto: all for one and one for all."

"Right." Chris swapped one of his skis with J.R. "Besides, who else would I trade skis with?" He took the odd pair over to the far side of the rack and tucked them out of sight.

"No wonder you ski weird," Greg Forbes said as Chris was about to go inside. "Your skis are two different sizes."

Chris decided to ignore the comment, and besides he didn't want to give away his secret to the enemy. It was bad enough that Greg knew where one of his skis was.

Chapter 14

SABOTAGE

"This is the way it looks now," Gadget said, making the final tabulations in the High-Fives' blue spiral note-book. The gang hovered over a small table inside Snoasis. "We ended up with a grand total of four minutes and seventeen seconds and the Raiders have four minutes and eleven seconds."

"A difference of six seconds," Chris said.

"It seems like so little, but I guess it's a lot when you figure how hard it is to do," Jack added.

Gadget made another tabulation. "We each have to shave over a second off our times this next run."

"And hope the Raiders make some mistakes," Stretch added.

"They ended up with two golds, one silver, and one bronze," J.R. said.

"We've got one gold and three silvers," Chris added.

Stretch looked out the window. "Too bad we can't use Alex's gold—she looked great."

J.R. lowered his head, feeling guilty. "Maybe she could wear my ski gear and take my place in the second run."

"No way, you'll be getting a gold of your own," Chris said.

"What's our plan for the next run?" Gadget asked.

"We need to keep a few things in mind," Chris explained. "Get an early weight shift off the outside edge quickly. Soften the slap of the ski it adds time and then hop to be quick. It sounds easy but it's tough to do."

"We can do it." Stretch snap-popped his fingers.

"You bet we can," Jack added.

"Let's get our gear on and head back up," Chris suggested after they'd finished their hot chocolate. "We can practice the human slalom course until it's time to race again." The gang jumped up with renewed determination and headed outside again.

"Something's wrong with my bindings," Chris exclaimed, testing his quick release. He stomped his foot again and the ski bounced off for the third time. He examined it closely to find a small screw missing. "Someone's been messing with my equipment."

"What do you mean?" J.R. asked.

"Unless I can find that screw, I don't have any skis."

"Sabotage." Stretch gasped.

Suddenly Chris remembered that Greg had watched him stash his skis. "I'll bet Forbes did it. He saw me leave them here."

"That's playing dirty," Jack snarled.

"What are you going to do? You don't have time to get it fixed," Gadget said.

"This is cheating," Jack growled.

"Yeah, but none of us saw him do it, so we can't prove a thing," J.R. added.

"You can use my skis," Stretch exclaimed. "We'll explain everything to the officials, and tell them you can't run your heat until I've finished the race."

"It might work," Gadget said hopefully. "But what if my boots don't fit in your bindings?"

Stretch shrugged. "You'll have to wear my boots and wear another pair of socks to make your feet wider."

"This is terrible," Jack said. "How are we going to beat the Raiders this way?"

"I don't think we have any choice," Gadget added.

"Look, just do the best you can. If we don't win, we can ask for a rematch," Stretch said.

"This stinks," Chris groaned. "You guys better get going. I'll wait here until Stretch can come in for the trade." The others nodded, and Chris paced back and forth in the snow.

It seemed like an eternity before the first pairing of High-Fives and Raiders skied down the slope. Chris was there to cheer Gadget on. Gadget was racing against Greg and this time he had his goggles on. "Think light on your feet," Chris called, coaching Gadget. Gadget skated out of the last gate and poled his way over the finish line. He'd made up one second, scoring forty-six seconds—another silver. Greg, on the other hand got another gold at forty-five seconds. It was a close and encouraging start.

"Way to go." Chris congratulated Gadget. "Who's up next?"

"Jack and Hank," Gadget replied. "Jack should take him, I hope." For a moment Jack almost fell. "Hop into it," Chris shouted. Amazingly Jack righted himself and he and Hank finished with identical fifty-second scores and silver medals.

"It's going to get harder with each run, isn't it?" Gadget asked.

"Yep," Chris said, kicking the snow with his boot. "If I ever get the truth out of Forbes, I'll kill him."

"Look, here comes Alex." Jack pointed her out as she gracefully cut the course with her edges. Again she received a gold, and again the guys wished they could use her time.

"All right, hold your breath—here comes J.R." Jack had turned his attention to his brother.

Secretly, Jack and Gadget and Chris crossed their fingers for a great run for J.R. "Lean and hop, lean and hop," Chris whispered, visualizing the course for him. Since J.R. and Peter had had the worst two times in the last heat, it was hard to tell if J.R. was faster or if Peter was having a slow run. But when J.R. schussed over the finish line, he had a bronze medal at fifty-five seconds.

"Now that's what I call improvement," the announcer called. "This competitor bettered his time by seventeen seconds. I don't know what you did, kid, but it worked."

The High-Fives went wild congratulating J.R. It was a win no matter what happened in the final two races. Each High-Five had won a medal. Peter had also improved, but only by three seconds. He won a bronze, too.

"What did you do to make such a difference?" Gadget asked.

"You switched your edges faster, right?" Jack quizzed.

"You leaned farther toward the fall line?" Chris added.

"Nope," J.R. said, grinning from ear to ear. "It was even simpler than that. I hummed my favorite song to myself."

Chris laughed and patted J.R. on the back. "Great job."

Gadget quickly scribbled down the times in the notebook. "We're behind by one second on this run, and we still need to make up six seconds from the first run in order to tie."

"Tie, heck, we want to win," Jack shouted.

Stretch and Randy came next, and Stretch was obviously the better skier. Chris was so nervous, he watched the whole race holding his breath. Stretch caught an edge and was three seconds slower than his first trial. He got a silver with forty-six seconds. Randy increased his time, but only by two seconds. Now, with the times from both runs combined, the Raiders were ahead by only one second.

Chris had never felt so much pressure. He had to make up that one lousy second and beat Ron by a margin of at least one more second. Stretch jumped out of his skis, and Chris, who had decided to wear his own boots, slid in. His father's advice echoed: "Safety first." Chris twisted and jumped, trying to release the ski. It stayed firm.

"Maybe you should try my boots," Stretch said.

"It's going to be a toss-up either way," Chris grumbled. "My feet are so narrow, they'd swim around in your boots. I can't get control that way. My best shot is to wear my boots and pray I don't fall. I don't have the weight to spring the release, so if I go, the skis may not come off, and that could be serious."

"I don't think you should risk it," Gadget said.

"He's right, we should forfeit," J.R. pleaded.

"I can't," Chris said with a lump in his throat. "It's me against Porter and I've got to come up with two seconds on Ron for us to win."

Stretch shook his head. "It's not worth getting hurt."

"The physical hurt won't be as bad as the mental injury if I don't race."

The gang was silent. They knew Chris had thought it through, and nothing was going to change his mind. Chris finished getting ready. "Wish me luck," he called, pushing off for the chair lift and the final run of the race.

Again Chris mentally prepared for the race. He was more nervous than ever. The skis felt so different, he actually wished he had his old Head XRs. They wouldn't fail him. If I hadn't made such a big deal about the K-2's, he thought, this whole mess could have been diverted. "Well, it's too late now," he muttered. "I've got to do it with what I've got."

Ron was waiting for him at the top, a mischievous

grin on his face. "There's no way you can win it, tough guy. I guess your K-2's failed you."

Chris glared back. "Yeah, maybe, but my friends didn't."

"Remember that, when you're carrying my gear to the bus."

"Don't count on it yet."

The official began the countdown, and Chris could hear the numbers bouncing off his stomach. "And *go*," the official called.

Chris hesitated for a minute, hoping Ron would push off first. He remembered that the clock wouldn't start until after his skis tripped the wand. If Porter was in front of him, he could keep him in sight. He didn't trust him. When Chris finally started he felt uneven but strong. His own advice rang through his head. Halfway through the first run he lifted his inside ski into the air, then *smack,* he transferred the pressure to it. He'd successfully shifted his weight early, rolling onto the edge, and then, prepared to raise the other ski, accelerating into each turn. His rhythm was strong and he found himself humming as he met the next gate. Ron was no longer on his mind. Suddenly something was wrong, though, dreadfully wrong. Porter was skiing within inches of him and Chris's timing went haywire. His ski tips crossed and it took all his effort not to tumble. He didn't fall, but it cost him several seconds to recover—seconds the High-Fives didn't have. When he crossed the finish line his time was the same as it had been before, forty-six seconds and a silver. Ron had done it in forty-five, a second more than his previous run, but the Raiders had won the whole grudge match by two seconds.

"You did your best." Gadget tried to make him feel better.

"We'll get them next time," Stretch added, and pounded Chris on the back.

Chris couldn't shake the feeling that he'd let the High-Fives down and now he'd have to put up with the Raiders' bragging, too. It was almost too much to bear.

"Meet you at the bottom, losers," Ron said. "I hope you're feeling strong because I brought lots of gear with me today."

The High-Fives were silent as the Raiders continued harassing them.

"Let's get out of here," Jack whispered.

"No," Chris said. "We have medals to accept, so we'll wait for the final results to be posted."

"We don't have to," Stretch added.

"Yes, we do," Chris fired back. "Maybe we didn't win the bet, but we did win medals, and I'm going to enjoy mine."

It seemed like hours before they posted the final results. The wait was well worth it.

"It must be a misprint," Ron shouted. "The clock said forty-five seconds."

The High-Fives were stunned. Next to Ron's name for the final run was the word *Disqualified*. He'd get no time or medal for that run.

"He went off course trying to mess Chris up," Jack said. "They caught him at it, too."

"Cheaters never prosper," Gadget added.

"I can't believe this," J.R. exclaimed.

"Neither can I, but I'm not arguing," Chris said.

"Now I wish I'd worn my steel-plated boots for Forbes to carry." Stretch whooped with delight.

The High-Fives' frustration turned to elation, and the gang did one of their special high-fives to celebrate. It was the perfect ending to a day of ups and downs. The Raiders grumbled and demanded a rematch as they staggered under all of the High-Fives' equipment, which included Stretch's snow board and Gadget's cross-country skis. Chris couldn't stop smiling the whole bus trip back to Conrad. He clutched his two silver medals proudly. He may not have won the gold, but he still felt as if he'd won the prize: the friendship of the High-Fives.

About the Author

S. S. GORMAN grew up in Greeley, Colorado, with two older brothers and two younger brothers. The family was always active in sports. Their favorites include skiing, skating, softball, golf, tennis, swimming, hiking, fishing, basketball, and football. Ms. Gorman has a B.S. degree from Colorado State University and an M.A. from the University of Northern Colorado. For the past fifteen years she has worked as a professional performer onstage and in radio and film, as well as written several young-adult novels. The titles in *The High-Fives* series are: *Soccer Is a Kick, Slam Dunk, Home Run Stretch, Quarterback Sneak,* and *Skiing for the Prize,* available from Minstrel Books. She currently lives in California with her husband and two children.

THE HIGH-FIVES™

by S.S. Gorman

JOIN
THE HIGH FIVES
AS THEY PLAY
TOGETHER TO WIN!